"I suppose being spoiled by a man is nice," Mellie said.

She held Case's probing stare. "But most women I know want to take care of themselves."

For the first time, she saw a shadow of cynicism on his face.

Mellie stood abruptly, feeling out of her depth and alarmingly sympathetic toward the man who'd been born and reared with every possible advantage. "I really do have to get busy."

Case unfolded that long, lean body and joined her at the dishwasher, his hands brushing hers as he put his plate alongside her cup. "Is your boss such a slave driver?" he muttered.

They were almost in an embrace, the counter at her back and one big, contrary cowboy planted in front of her. "*I'm* the boss, Case. And I don't need to be spoiled. If I want to fly to Paris this weekend, I'll buy my own damned ticket."

His gaze settled on her lips. For one heart-thumping second she knew he was going to kiss her. "You just told me I'm not your boss. We're here as equals, Mellie. So I guess whatever happens, happens."

* * *

Courting the Cowboy Boss is part of the Texas Cattleman's Club: Lies and Lullabies series—Baby secrets and a scheming sheikh rock Royal, Texas.

Dear Reader,

Have you ever wondered who cleans Taylor Swift's house? I think of weird things like that and wonder about the issues of security and anonymity. Famous people are vulnerable in many ways. How do they know whom they can trust?

My hero is not *famous* famous, but he definitely is a big deal in Texas, and particularly in the town of Royal. I understand his reluctance to open his home to a stranger.

I hope you'll enjoy this story of two very different people who share a mutual attraction and who find that in our weakest moments we sometimes stumble upon something very special.

Happy reading,

Janice Maynard

COURTING THE COWBOY BOSS

———

JANICE MAYNARD

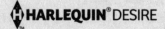

Special thanks and acknowledgment are given to Janice Maynard for her contribution to the Texas Cattleman's Club: Lies and Lullabies miniseries.

ISBN-13: 978-0-373-73422-1

Courting the Cowboy Boss
Copyright © 2015 by Harlequin Books S.A.

Reclaimed by the Rancher
Copyright © 2015 by Harlequin Books S.A.

PLEASE RECYCLE
THIS PRODUCT IS RECYCLABLE

Recycling programs
for this product may
not exist in your area.

This edition published by arrangement with Harlequin Books S.A.

For questions and comments about the quality of this book, please contact us at CustomerService@Harlequin.com.

Printed in U.S.A.

HARLEQUIN®
www.Harlequin.com

CONTENTS

USA TODAY bestselling author **Janice Maynard** knew she loved books and writing by the time she was eight years old. But it took multiple rejections and many years of trying before she sold her first three novels. After teaching kindergarten and second grade for a number of years, Janice turned in her lesson plan book and began writing full-time. Since then she has sold over thirty-five books and novellas. Janice lives in east Tennessee with her husband, Charles. They love hiking, traveling and spending time with family.

Hearing from readers is one of the best perks of the job!

You can connect with Janice at twitter.com/janicemaynard, facebook.com/janicemaynardreaderpage, wattpad.com/user/janicemaynard and instagram.com/janicemaynard.

Books by Janice Maynard

HARLEQUIN DESIRE

Texas Cattleman's Club: Lies and Lullabies

Courting the Cowboy Boss

The Kavanaghs of Silver Glen

A Not-So-Innocent Seduction
Baby for Keeps
Christmas in the Billionaire's Bed
Twins on the Way
Second Chance with the Billionaire

Visit the Author Profile page at Harlequin.com, or janicemaynard.com, for more titles.

COURTING THE
COWBOY BOSS
Janice Maynard

For Jamie and Daniel, who have made Texas
their home...we miss you in Tennessee!

One

"To our new president!"

Three of the four men at the table lifted their glasses in a semicongratulatory toast. Case Baxter, the object of their wry tribute, shook his head and grinned. "Thanks, guys. You're all heart."

Mac McCallum finished off the last bite of his Angus burger and wiped his mouth with a linen napkin. "Seriously, man. What were you thinking? You're like all the rest of us...up to your ears in work. Adding president of the Texas Cattleman's Club to your résumé means more headaches."

Mac was CEO of McCallum Energy...and understood as much as anybody that success was a double-edged sword. Even so, with his big laugh and extrovert ways, he always seemed laid-back and easygoing.

Though the formal dining room at the Texas Cattleman's Club was an elegant venue, the majority of the diners were men like Mac and Case. Tough, honed by physical labor,

perpetually tanned by the hot Texas sun. And wealthy...
wealthy enough to think they had the world on a string.

Case shrugged. "I know what you're saying. And you're
right. But when the committee asked to put my name on
the ballot, I could hear my great-grandfather cheering from
the grave. It's an honor. And a privilege."

His companions hooted with laughter. Jeff Hartley
wiped his eyes. "Of course it is. No denying that. But unless you have some magic formula for adding an extra eight
or ten hours to every day, I'm not exactly sure how you're
going to manage." Jeff owned and operated the Hartley
Cattle Ranch. He knew more than a little about hard work
and long days.

Case had an ominous feeling in his gut that said his buddies were right. The truth was, though, Case's family had
lived in Royal for generations. They believed in tradition,
honor and service. He hadn't been able to bring himself to
say no to the nomination. Then again, he hadn't expected
to be elected. The other two candidates were older and, as
far as Case was concerned, more suited for the position.

But now it was too late for second thoughts. "I'm counting on the three of you to be my unofficial advisors."

Parker Reese leaned back in his chair. "Don't look at
me. I'm a doctor, not a rancher. I can get your baby through
colic, but all I know about cattle is not to wave a red flag
in front of a bull."

In the general laughter that followed, Case spared a moment to marvel at how things had changed. Not long ago,
women had finally been admitted into the hallowed halls
of the club as full members.

Times, they were a-changin'...

Case looked at Mac with a lifted brow. "I thought Logan
was joining us for lunch." Logan Wade was Mac's best
friend and one of his key investors.

"He bought three new horses last week," Mac said, "and they're being delivered today. You know how he is."

They all nodded. Horses and women. Logan's two favorite things.

Mac pinned Case with a knowing gaze. "Quit changing the subject. We were talking about you and your soon-to-be-impossible schedule."

"Gil Addison has a son and a wife," Case pointed out. "And he's been a great president. I'm blissfully single."

"True," Mac said. "You're forgetting, however, that Gil is Superman. No offense, buddy, but those are big shoes to fill."

"Your support is duly noted."

Parker, arguably the smartest man in the room, added his two cents' worth. "You've always liked a challenge, Case. Don't let them mess with your head. You've got this."

"Thanks." Case had enormous respect for the dedicated though reserved neonatal specialist. Royal's hospital was lucky to have a doctor of Parker's caliber on staff.

Jeff chimed in, mischief written all over his face. "Parker has more faith in you than I do. I've been in your house, Case. It's such a mess you can't even find the TV remote half the time. I'd suggest burning your place to the ground if we weren't in the middle of a drought."

Case's neck heated. Organization was not his strong suit. Another fact that called his ability to perform his newly acquired duties into question.

"I've already thought about that," he said. "And I have a plan."

Mac gave their waitress a smile as she brought their desserts. "Do tell."

Case stuck a fork in his apple cobbler. "I'm going to hire a housekeeper."

The other three men stared at him.

Mac lifted his spoonful of ice cream and waved it in

the air. "You do know she would have to come inside your house for that to work?"

"Very funny." Case squared his shoulders. "I have the Texas Cattleman's Club to run now. I have to make compromises."

Jeff still seemed shocked. "But what about your rule number one? *Never allow a female into the man cave.*"

"Unless she's a relative." Parker supplied the exception. "Is this new housekeeper a relative?"

Case deserved the inquisition. He was known for his only-half-joking rules for dealing with the female sex. When he was involved in intimate relationships, he preferred to spend the night at the woman's home. So he could leave when he wanted to. "I made the rules," he said, his chin thrust out. "And I can change them. This woman will be a stranger…an employee. She won't be a relative, but she might as well be. I'm not hiring a woman—I'm hiring a housekeeper."

He gave them a warning scowl. "I've learned from my mistakes, believe me." The men at the table knew the unsavory details of Case's not-so-happy marriage. He'd had a fling with his family's accountant, married her and soon found out that she was more interested in spending Case's money than in being a loving wife. It was a salutary lesson.

Jeff turned down a second beer but took a long swig of his water. "Hey, man. A guy's gotta do what a guy's gotta do. And besides, up until the tornado last year, this club-president gig wasn't all that onerous. You'll be fine."

Everyone nodded, but Case saw his own reservations reflected on their faces. Ever since the F4 tornado that had decimated Maverick County and the town of Royal barely over a year ago, the Texas Cattleman's Club had become one of the anchors that held things together.

Coordinating rescue efforts, keeping up morale, apply-

ing for grants, planning reconstruction and renovation—
the club and its president had served the people of Royal
well. Life was mostly back to normal, but there was still
work to be done. So Case couldn't kid himself into thinking that his new job title was ceremonial only.

Jeff interrupted the momentary silence. "If we're finished raking Case over the coals, I have a serious subject to
bring up. Shouldn't we be worried about all the ranches and
other parcels of land that have been sold in Royal lately?
And almost all of it to a single buyer? Does anybody but
me think it's a little odd?"

Mac shrugged. "I'm not really concerned. A number of
people were demoralized by the storm or too strapped for
cash to rebuild. It sounds like they're getting good offers
and the chance to start over somewhere else."

Parker's brow furrowed. "I hadn't heard about this."

Case nodded. "Nolan Dane is back in town and is rep-
resenting a company called Samson Oil in these acquisi-
tions. It doesn't make sense to me, though. Why would
an oil company be interested in the land? The tracts he's
buying up were checked for oil decades ago." Nolan was
raised in Royal, but had been gone for a long time.

"Maybe they're planning to use some of the newer technology and hoping to get lucky," Mac said.

Jeff shook his head. "Nolan seems like a decent guy, but
I'm not a big fan of lawyers, particularly when someone
else is hiding behind that lawyer's legal speak."

"We should give him the benefit of the doubt," Parker
said. "At least as long as the people selling are getting a
fair shake. It seems to me that Case will be in a perfect
position to keep tabs on this kind of thing."

Case glanced at his watch. "Speaking of my upcoming
lifestyle change, I have an appointment in forty-five minutes to interview my new domestic assistant."

"Is that the politically correct term these days?" Jeff seemed dubious.

Parker scrawled his name on the check, charging it to his club account as was their custom. "I think Case is trying to convince himself that a woman won't ruin his carefully preserved chaos."

Mac nodded, his grin broad. "I never met a woman yet who didn't want to domesticate a man. No matter how old she is."

Case lifted an eyebrow. "I am the newly elected president of a venerable organization whose members have run this town for over a century. I think I can handle a housekeeper." He stood, and his friends followed suit.

Mac shook his hand. "You can count on me in the days ahead, sir."

Case grinned. "Bite me."

Parker saluted. "Happy to serve under your command."

Jeff bowed. "*Mi casa es su casa* if you need a place to hide out."

"Everybody's a comedian." As Case said his goodbyes and headed out to the parking lot, he reminded himself what a lucky man he was. He had a ranch and land he loved, a wide circle of friends, and now the respect and a nod of confidence from his peers who had voted for him.

If he could iron out this housekeeper thing, no pun intended, his life would be under control.

Mellie Winslow took in the sights as she made her way down the long driveway leading to the B Hive Ranch. Case Baxter's fields and fences were immaculate, several varieties of placid cattle grazing peacefully as far as the eye could see. She envied him the order and success of his thriving operation.

Though her own small business, the Keep N Clean, was

doing well, it couldn't compare to the prosperity of this massive endeavor. Case must be an extraordinarily busy man—hence his request for a housekeeper.

Mellie knew that a good word from Case Baxter could be a boon to her business. What she didn't know was whether or not Case would accept her proposition.

When at last she pulled up in front of the charming ranch house that had housed generations of Baxter men and their families, she noticed something odd. Apparently, Case's cattle received more attention than did his aging home.

It would be an exaggeration to say the place looked run-down. That wasn't it at all. But the two-story white ranch house with blue shutters seemed tired. Although the wraparound porch was large and appealing, no flowers were planted at its base. No colorful cushions bedecked the porch swing. No toddler bicycles or teen sports equipment lay scattered about the yard.

Although the B Hive Ranch had been in the family for decades, everyone in Royal knew that Case's parents had both died young, and Case was an only child. It would be sad to see the place end up in other hands if Case had no heirs.

It was a possibility, though. Case was in his midthirties and apart from—or perhaps because of—his youthful marriage, which had ended badly, he showed no signs of settling down.

Taking a deep breath to steady her nerves, Mellie reminded herself that this was not her first rodeo. Keep N Clean had just celebrated its eighth anniversary. Mellie herself was a seasoned businesswoman. There was no need to feel intimidated by the power and stature of Case Baxter.

She didn't know him well. Really only in passing.

Hopefully, that was about to change.

Along with her stylish tote that served as purse and catchall, she picked up a navy-and-lime-green folder that she now handed out to all prospective clients. Though the expense of producing the upscale advertising materials had been wince-worthy, she hoped the professional presentation would take her expanding company to the next level.

For some reason, she'd expected someone other than the owner to answer her knock. But only seconds passed before the tall blue-eyed man with dark brown hair opened the door and swung it wide.

He greeted her with a polite smile. "I'm Case Baxter. I'm assuming you're here for the interview?" He filled the doorway, lean and long and wildly handsome.

Mellie shook his hand, feeling his large, warm fingers momentarily squeeze hers. *Wow.* His photograph in the newspaper didn't do him justice. His short hair was neatly cut, though an unshaven chin gave him a rakish air. His clasp was not a second too long. Nothing out of the ordinary.

But her heart beat faster.

He was the perfect specimen of a Texas male. He wore faded jeans that molded to his body in interesting ways… scuffed hand-tooled cowboy boots, a cotton shirt with the sleeves rolled up and an expensive watch that looked as if it could pick up cable channels on Mars.

She found her voice at last. "I'm Mellie Winslow. I own Keep N Clean."

Case frowned slightly. He didn't invite her in. "I thought I was interviewing a prospective housekeeper."

"Well, you are," she said, squirming inwardly. "The truth is, Mr. Baxter, I've been expanding my business. Things are going very well. But when you called asking for help, I decided I wanted to take this job myself."

"Why?"

It was a valid question. She decided that honesty was the way to go. "May I come in so we can talk about it?"

"I supposed so." He led her into the adjoining dining room, where a large formal table groaned beneath the weight of stacks of mail. In the few places not covered by papers, a layer of dust coated the wood.

"Have a seat," he said. "As you can see, I didn't exaggerate my need for assistance."

Mellie sat down, and when he did the same, she slid a Keep N Clean folder across the table. "My rates and services are all listed here. The reason I'd like to do this job myself, Mr. Baxter, is because all of my current staff have taken on as much as they can handle. But I don't want to turn you away. Having the newly elected president of the Texas Cattleman's Club as a client would be invaluable advertising."

"Always assuming you're as good as you say..." He opened the folder and scanned testimonials she'd included from satisfied clients.

Mellie frowned. "I'm a hard worker. I'm meticulous. Also, I don't need anyone to hold my hand every moment. Once you tell me what you require and give me detailed instructions about what I should and should not muck with in your home, I'll be invisible."

Case leaned back in his chair, folded his arms across his chest and stared at her.

She refused to fidget. If this silent showdown was part of his interview strategy, she would pass muster or die trying.

At last he shrugged. "Your rates seem fair. But how do you propose to run your business and at the same time keep my house in order?"

"How do you propose to run *your* business and still keep the TCC in order?"

Sarcasm was one of her failings. Having a smart mouth was not the way to win over prospective clients. Fortunately for her, Case Baxter laughed.

His eyes went from glacial blue to sunshiny skies when he was amused. "Touché." He tapped the fingers of one hand on the table, the small restless gesture indicating some level of dissatisfaction or concern.

Mellie leaned forward, giving him her best reassuring smile. "Have you used another service that wasn't up to par? We could talk about where they fell short."

"No." His jaw tensed for a moment as if some distasteful memory had unsettled him. "I don't tolerate strangers in my home very well. I like my privacy."

"That's understandable. If you prefer, we can arrange for me to clean when you're gone. Or maybe that's the idea you don't like. I could make sure to work while you're here. Whatever it takes, Mr. Baxter. How about a month's trial run? At the end of that time, if you're unhappy with the quality of my work, or if having someone come in to clean bothers you too much, I'll cancel the contract with no penalty."

"I can see why your business is doing well. It's hard to say no to you."

Mellie saw a definite twinkle in his eyes. She flushed. "I'm ambitious. But I think a man like you understands that. You won't regret having me here, Mr. Baxter, I promise. In fact, I swear you'll wonder why you didn't hire Keep N Clean a lot sooner."

"Perhaps I should be absolutely clear. It's more than cleaning. If you come to work for me, I'll want you to take a shot at organizing my home life."

His request wasn't out of the ordinary. Structuring a client's daily environment to maximize family time and personal efficiency was something Mellie enjoyed. But it was hard to imagine Case Baxter allowing anyone, much less Mellie, access to something so personal.

When she hesitated, his eyes narrowed. "Is that a problem?"

"No. Not at all. But you mentioned protecting your privacy, so I would want to be perfectly clear about boundaries."

"Such as?"

She floundered mentally, oddly put off her game by a conversation that shouldn't have seemed the slightest bit provocative and yet drew her thoughts to sex-tossed sheets and whether Case Baxter favored boxers or briefs.

"There are many levels of organization, Mr. Baxter. Everything from creating a well-aligned sock drawer to alphabetizing kitchen spices."

He chuckled, ratcheting up his masculine appeal at least a hundredfold. "I'm sure we can settle somewhere between the two."

"So that's a yes?" She cocked her head, her stomach a swirl of anticipation and feminine interest. Mixing business with pleasure had never been an issue, but with this man, she might have to be on her guard. He had neither said nor done anything to acknowledge the fact that she was a woman and he was a man. But it was kind of a hard thing to miss.

He nodded. "I think it's a workable compromise. We'll see how we get along together. And in the meantime, if you find that one of your other staff members is free to take over here, I'll certainly understand."

"Does that mean you don't want me?"

Sweet holy Hannah. Where had that come from?

Two

His body tightened, on high alert. Though he was almost certain Mellie Winslow hadn't intended anything suggestive by her question, there was enough of a spark in the air to make him react with a man's natural response to a beautiful available woman.

Case hadn't expected the punch of sexual interest. Truth be told, it reinforced his reservations about hiring any housekeeper, much less one who looked like Mellie. He was a sucker for redheads, especially the kind with skin the color of cream and wide emerald eyes reflecting a certain wariness…as if she had been disappointed one too many times in life.

Though she was clearly accustomed to hard physical labor, she was thin but not skinny. The shade of her red curls, spilling from a ponytail that fell past her shoulders, was a combination of fire and sunshine.

He should tell her to go. Right now.

"Are you saying I make you nervous, Ms. Winslow?"

She wrinkled her nose, as if smelling a refrigerator full of rotten eggs. "A little. I suppose. But I'll get over it."

That last sentence was served with a side of feminine defiance designed to put him in his place. She reminded him of a fluffy chicken warning the rooster away from the henhouse.

"Duly noted." He tapped a stack of envelopes. "The trial period works both ways. You may find me such a slob that you'll run screaming for the hills."

Mellie's smile was open and natural. "I doubt that. I've reformed worse offenders than you, believe me."

At that precise moment, he knew he wasn't imagining the sizzle of physical awareness between them. Maybe Mellie didn't notice, but he did. At thirty-six, he surely had more experience than this young woman, who was on the dewy-skinned right side of thirty.

"Don't say I didn't warn you." He glanced at his watch, ruefully aware that he had to put an end to this provocative interview. "I'm afraid I have another appointment in town. So we'll have to wrap this up. Why don't you plan to start Thursday morning? I'll put some thoughts on paper in regard to what I want you to tackle and we can go from there. Does that work for you?"

Mellie stood, smiling. "Absolutely. Thank you, Mr. Baxter. I'll see you soon."

"Call me Case," he said.

"And I'm Mellie."

Case stood at the window, his hand on the lace curtain as he watched his new housekeeper drive away. He knew the time had come to put his house in order—literally—but he had a sinking feeling that he might be making a bad mistake.

The fact that he found Mellie Winslow so appealing

should have put an end to things. He'd fallen for an employee once before and ended up with a broken marriage and a bank account that had taken a severe hit. His track record with long-term relationships was virtually nonexistent.

He'd never had sisters. With his mother gone, the only female relatives he had were two cousins in California whom he saw maybe once a decade. He wasn't a good judge of what made women tick. He enjoyed their company in bed. He was even willing to concede that women and men could be friends under certain circumstances.

But as one of the wealthiest ranchers in Maverick County, he'd learned the hard way that a man was not always judged on his own merits. He might marry again one day…maybe. But only if he was damn sure that his prospective bride cared more about his character than his financial bottom line.

As he drove into town, he noted, almost unconsciously, the signs that Royal was flourishing after last fall's F4 tornado. He took in the new storefronts, fresh landscaping and a few empty lots where damaged buildings had been razed in preparation for upcoming construction.

The town had rebounded well, despite tragedy and hardship. Case knew there were still problems to be addressed. Insurance woes remained an issue. Slow payments. Court battles over settlements. The Texas Cattleman's Club had a history of benevolence and community service. Case was determined to use his new position to keep the organization headed in the right direction, particularly in regard to the ongoing tornado cleanup.

For Royal to rebound from tragedy and prosper in the twenty-first century, it would be important to keep all sectors of the local economy alive. Which meant looking out for small businesses. Like the Keep N Clean.

When he pulled up on the side street adjoining the Royal Diner, he saw that the sheriff's squad car was already there. He found Nathan Battle inside, sipping a cup of coffee and flirting with his wife, Amanda, who owned and operated the diner.

Case took off his cowboy hat and tucked it under his left arm. "Sheriff. Amanda. Good to see you both." He shook Nathan's hand and slid into the booth opposite the tall uniformed man he'd come to meet.

Amanda smiled at him. "Congratulations on the election. I just heard the news."

"Thanks." Nathan and Amanda had been high school sweethearts. After a tough breakup as kids, they'd eventually reconnected, fallen in love all over again and married. Case envied the almost palpable intimacy between them. Two people who had known each other for so long didn't have to worry about secrets or betrayals.

Amanda kissed her husband on the cheek. "You boys have fun. I've got to go track down a missing shipment of flour, so Helen will be your waitress today. I'll catch you later."

The server took their order for coffee and dessert, and Case sat back with a sigh. He worked long hours. His daddy had taught him the ranching business from the ground up and drilled into him the notion that in order to be the boss, a man required more than money in the bank. He needed the respect and loyalty of his employees.

Nathan drained his coffee cup and raised a hand for more.

Case shook his head. "Do you live on that stuff?" Nathan was tall and lean and beloved by most of the town. But he rarely had time for leisure.

The sheriff shrugged. "There are worse vices." He smiled at Helen as she gave him a refill, and then he eyed

Case with curiosity. "What's up, Case? You sounded mysterious on the phone."

Case leaned forward. "No mystery. I'm hoping you'll be available to look over the club's security procedures and disaster plans. Last year's tornado taught us all we need to stay on top of emergency preparedness."

"Not a bad idea. I'd be happy to…just email me some dates and times, and I'll block it off on my calendar."

"Thanks. I appreciate it."

They chatted for half an hour, and then almost as an afterthought, Case asked Nathan the question that had been on his mind. "What do you know about Keep N Clean?"

"Mellie Winslow's business?"

"Yes."

"They're a solid outfit. Amanda has used them here at the diner, and I know a lot of people around town who sing their praises. Why?"

"My housekeeper retired eight months ago. Took her pension and headed to Florida. I need help around the house. Especially now that I'm taking on leadership at the club. But I'm out on the ranch a lot of the time, and I don't like the idea of having strangers invade my personal space."

"I'm sure Mellie vets her employees thoroughly. I've never heard a single complaint about anyone on her staff, and I would know if there had been a problem."

"And Mellie herself? She says her staffing situation is stretched to the max, so she would be the one working for me."

The other man obviously knew about Case's short-lived marriage. It was no secret. But it was humiliating nevertheless. Back then, Case had been thinking with a part of his anatomy other than his brain. The resultant debacle had been a tough lesson for a twentysomething.

Nathan raised an eyebrow. "Are you asking as a boss or as a man?"

"What does that mean?" Case hadn't expected to be grilled.

"Well, Melinda Winslow is not only a savvy business-woman, she's a gorgeous unattached redhead who's smart and funny and would be a great companion for any guy."

"Hell, Nathan." Case took a swig of coffee and nearly choked to death when the hot liquid singed his throat. "Why do all of my married friends feel the need to play matchmaker?"

Nathan grinned. "How many times have *you* gotten laid in the last month?"

"Not all marriages are like yours," Case muttered, refusing to be jealous of his buddy's good fortune. "Amanda is a peach."

"So is Mellie. Don't let your prejudices get in the way. And to be clear, *now* I'm talking about business again. She can be trusted, Case…if that's what you're asking. You can relax on that score. She's not going to steal the silver or run off with a Picasso."

Case's parents had been art collectors. The ranch house was filled with priceless paintings and sculptures. "Good to know. I liked her during the interview, but it never hurts to get a second opinion. Anything else you want to add to your glowing recommendation?"

Something flickered across Nathan's face…something that gave Case a moment's pause. "What?" Case asked, mildly alarmed.

"Nothing bad about Mellie. But be on your guard if her dad comes around. He's a drunk and a scoundrel. As far as I can tell, fathering Mellie is the only good thing he ever did. I arrest the guy for public intoxication at least several times a year."

"And Mellie supports him?"

"No. He lives off the rents from a handful of properties around town that have been in the Winslow family for generations. In fact, the Texas Cattleman's Club sits on Winslow's land. Mellie helps out with the leasing company now and then, but I think she started her own business in order to keep as far away from him as possible."

"No mother in the picture?"

"She died a long time ago. I imagine she left her daughter some kind of nest egg that allowed Mellie to start her business. The family used to be financially solvent, but Mellie's dad has almost destroyed everything. Booze mostly, but gambling, too."

"Thanks for the heads-up." After taking a bite of pie, Case moved on to another subject. "What do you know about Samson Oil and their connection to Nolan Dane? I hear he's handling a lot of land sales for them."

Nathan nodded. "I've heard it, too. Dane seems a decent sort. And his roots are here. So I assume he's trustworthy. Still, Samson Oil is not a household name. No one seems to know much about them."

"Do me a favor and keep an eye on Dane and the Samson Oil situation. Something about that whole thing seems a little off to me…"

Thursday morning Case found himself pacing the halls of his way-too-big-for-one-man house. At least half a dozen times he'd pulled out his phone to call Mellie Winslow and cancel her services. But he couldn't think of a single explanation that wouldn't make him sound like a paranoid idiot, so he'd resisted the impulse to wave her off.

Relishing his privacy was one thing. But if he continued to keep women out of his house, he'd wind up a withered, curmudgeonly octogenarian with a fortune in the because he needed to grow up, become responsible and make something out of himself. She deserved a man who could be all that he could be, and after he'd accomplished that goal he would come for her. Sitting on the edge of the bed now, she flipped through the album, which she had dedicated to Bane. She thought of him often. Every day. What she tried not to think about was why it was taking him so long to come back for her, or how he might be somewhere enjoying life without her. Forcing those thoughts from her mind, she packed the album in her luggage.

Moments later, she had rolled her luggage into the living room and was calling for a cab when her doorbell rang.

She went still. Nobody ever visited her. Who would be doing so now? She crept back into the shadows of her hallway, hoping whoever was at the door would think she wasn't home. She held her breath when the doorbell sounded again. Did the person on the other side know she was there?

She rushed into her bedroom and grabbed her revolver out of the nightstand drawer. By the time she'd made it back to the living room, there was a second knock. She moved toward the door, but stopped five feet away. "Who is it?" She tightened her hands on the revolver.

There was a moment of silence. And then a voice said, "It's me, Crystal. Bane."

Bane will do whatever it takes to keep his woman safe, but will it be enough?

Don't miss BANE by New York Times bestselling author Brenda Jackson. Available December 2015 wherever Harlequin® Desire books and ebooks are sold.

www.Harlequin.com

HARLEQUIN **Desire**™

Bane Westmoreland and Crystal Newsome secretly eloped when they were young—but then their families tore them apart. Now, five years later, Bane is coming back for his woman, and no one will stop him.

*Read on for a sneak peek of BANE the final book in **Brenda Jackson's THE WESTMORELAND** series*

With her heart thundering hard in her chest, Crystal began throwing items in the suitcase open on her bed. Had she imagined it or had she been watched when she'd entered her home tonight? She had glanced around several times and hadn't noticed anything or anyone. But still...

She took a deep breath, knowing she couldn't lose her cool. She made a decision to leave her car here and a few lights burning inside her house to give the impression she was home. She would call a cab to take her to the airport and would take only the necessities and a few items of clothing. She could buy anything else she needed.

But this, she thought as she studied the photo album she held in her hand, went everywhere with her. She had purchased it right after her last phone call with Bane. Her parents had sent Crystal to live with Aunt Rachel to finish out the last year of school. They wanted to get her away from Bane, not knowing she and Bane had secretly married.

A couple of months after she left Denver, she'd gotten a call from him. He'd told her he'd enlisted in the navy

bank and a cold, lonely existence. Still…old habits were hard to break.

Mellie arrived five minutes before their arranged appointment time. He'd have to give her points right off the bat for promptness. When he opened the door at her knock, he blinked momentarily.

It could have been a reaction to the blinding midmorning sun. But more probably, it was the sight of a slender, smiling woman in knee-length navy shorts and a navy knit top piped with lime green. On her feet she wore navy Keds with emerald laces.

The name of her business was embroidered above one breast. A breast that he didn't notice. Not at all.

He cleared his throat. "Come on in. I fixed us some iced tea." Though it was November, the day was extremely hot and muggy.

"Thank you." Mellie carried a large plastic tote loaded with various cleaning supplies.

"Leave that, why don't you? We'll sit down in the kitchen. I hope that's not too informal."

"Of course not."

Mellie seemed at ease when she took a seat. Thankfully, she tucked those long, tanned legs out of sight beneath the table. The back of his neck started to sweat. He wanted to get this over with as quickly as possible and get to work.

He sat down on the opposite side of the table and held out a piece of paper. "Here's a rundown of my priorities. Feel free to add things as you see anything that needs attention."

His newest employee glanced over the list. With her gaze cast downward, he could see how long her lashes were. "This looks good," she said. "I'll start out working full days for a couple of weeks until I get everything deep-

cleaned and organized. After that we can talk about how often you'd like me to come."

Case caught himself before his mind raced down a totally inappropriate path. Perhaps Nathan was right. Maybe Case *had* gone too long without sex. Because everything that came out of Mellie Winslow's mouth sounded like an invitation.

Case cleared his throat. "I was at the diner and saw Nathan the other day. The sheriff had good things to say about you and your business...that you were completely trustworthy."

"How did that come up in conversation? Were you investigating me?"

"No, no, no," he said, backpedaling rapidly. "But you can't fault me for asking what he knew about you."

She stood up, her expression going from affronted to glacial in seconds. "In the folder I gave you several days ago there were half a dozen references. Any one of those people could have vouched for me. It wasn't really a *police* matter, Mr. Baxter."

"I've offended you," he said, surprised at her reaction.

She tossed his list at him. "If you're going to constantly keep tabs to make sure I haven't cleaned out your safe or absconded with a priceless painting, then I don't think this is going to work out. Good day, Mr. Baxter."

Before he could react, she spun on her heel and headed for the front door, her ponytail bouncing with each angry step.

"Wait." Belatedly, he sprang to his feet and strode after her, whacking his hip on the corner of the kitchen table. "Wait, Mellie."

He caught up with her in the foyer as she picked up her supplies. "Don't leave," he said. "We agreed to a trial period."

"Shortest one on record," she snapped.

He really had no choice but to grab her arm in a gentle grip. "I'm *sorry*," he said…as forcefully as he knew how. "If you leave, I'll sue for breach of contract." He said it with a smile to let her know he was joking. But Mellie Winslow didn't look the least bit amused.

Wiggling free of his hold, she faced him, her expression turbulent. "I'm proud of my business. It's been built on word of mouth and the quality of the employees I hire. Keep N Clean has never had a single complaint of anything going missing…or of anything being damaged, for that matter."

Case rarely made a misstep, but he knew this was a bad one. "I am sincerely sorry. I shouldn't have asked the sheriff about you."

"Amanda Battle is a friend of mine. Do you understand that I'm embarrassed?"

He did. For the first time, he looked at his actions from Mellie's perspective. To a Texan, honor was everything. She had a right to be upset.

"Let's start over," he said.

She stared at him. "Under one condition. No trial period. You sign the contract today."

The negotiator in him was impressed. But more importantly, as a man, he found her bold confidence arousing. Everything about her was appealing. In other circumstances, he would have made an effort to get to know her more intimately.

Mellie Winslow, however, was here to put his house in order, not warm his bed. "I begin to see why your business is so successful. Very well, Ms. Winslow." He held out his hand. "You've got a deal."

Touching her was his next mistake. Awareness sizzled between them. Her skin was smooth and warm, her hand

small and feminine in his grasp. He maintained the contact a few seconds longer than necessary.

When he released her and she stepped back, for the first time, he saw uncertainty in her eyes. "I probably overreacted," she muttered. "I have a temper."

A grin tugged the corners of his mouth. "So the red hair is the real deal?"

"It is. I'm sorry, too. I shouldn't have been so touchy."

They stood there staring at each other, the air rife with things best left unspoken. "I should go," he said. "And let you get started."

She nodded. "If I have any questions, is it okay to text you?"

"Of course."

Her green eyes with a hint of gray warmed slightly. "I'll try not to bother you."

Too late for that. He picked up his keys from the table beside the front door. "See you later, Mellie Winslow. Good luck with my house."

Three

Mellie watched him go with mixed feelings. On the one hand, it was much easier to familiarize herself with a new house if the owner was not underfoot. Still, she wouldn't have minded if her new boss had lingered. She was curious about Case Baxter. Even though he was an arrogant, know-it-all male.

He was an intriguing combination of down-to-earth cowboy and high-powered businessman. It was no secret he was worth millions.

From what she'd heard around town, in addition to running his massive and wildly successful cattle operation, Case liked investing, particularly in small businesses. He believed in supporting the local economy. After the tornado—when the banks were stretched thin giving out loans—Case had floated some cash around the community, as well.

People in Royal liked and respected Case Baxter. Which explained his recent election as president of the Texas

Cattleman's Club. The newspaper had run a bio along with the article announcing the results. Mellie knew that Case was thirty-six, which made him seven years her senior.

The age gap wasn't significant, except for the fact that she still felt as though she was starting out, while Case was a man in his prime…in every way that counted.

Shrugging off her absorption with the sexy cowboy, she made herself focus on the job at hand. Case's home was a stunning example of what could happen when the past was carefully preserved even amidst modern improvements. Unfortunately, the beauty of the old house was obscured by clutter.

Judging by the kitchen, Case apparently grabbed only breakfast and lunch at home. Presumably, he ate dinner out most nights. She found orange juice and milk in the fridge and a couple of boxes of cereal in the cabinet. Lunch items were similarly sparse. Aside from pizzas and a couple of steaks in the freezer, his larder was woefully bare.

There was no reason in the world for her to feel sorry for Case Baxter. The man had everything he wanted or needed. He could hire a full-time chef if he liked. But the thought of him rattling around this big old house on his own gave her a twinge.

Not many men had the gift of making a home cozy and warm. Case was a Texas bachelor. Macho. Authoritative. Accustomed to giving orders and running his ranch. He wasn't the kind to bake cookies or pick flowers.

That mental image made her chuckle. Time to get to work.

She started with the dining room, since it seemed the most straightforward. Case had instructed her to pitch all the junk mail into the recycle bin and to keep only the things that looked personal or otherwise important. Though the stacks of envelopes, catalogs and circulars

were high, anybody with half a brain could sort through this kind of stuff in no time.

When she was done, there were maybe a dozen pieces of *real* mail remaining. She carried them down the hall and put them on Case's desk, a beautiful antique rolltop. His office was curiously impersonal. No knickknacks. No photographs, not even of his parents.

That was the thing about cleaning someone's house. It was an oddly intimate activity. She understood suddenly why a man like Case had been hesitant about hiring help. If the state of his home was any indication, he was a guarded man, one who didn't easily reveal his secrets.

By the time she made it to his bedroom, she had spent most of the day in only three rooms. That was no surprise, really. Decluttering was a slow process, especially when it involved someone else's belongings. But she had been successful. The living room and dining room were now spotless, as was Case's study.

It was past time for her to leave, so his bedroom would have to wait. But she did take a moment to gather discarded clothing and carry the items to the laundry room. Tomorrow that would be her first priority.

She paused in the doorway, lingering a moment, unable to help herself. The man's bed was hedonistic. An enormous carved four-poster that looked Spanish in origin dominated the room. No expense had been spared in the bed linens. The ecru sheets and thick, fluffy coffee-brown comforter were both masculine and luxurious.

The covers were tangled, as if their owner had passed a restless night. In the jumble of clothing she'd picked up off the floor and from a chair and in the bathroom, there were no pajamas. Maybe Case Baxter slept in the nude.

With her face hot and her stomach jumpy, Mellie went back and made the bed quickly before retreating, content

to leave this battlefield for another day. Never before had she taken such an intense interest in a client's sleeping arrangements. Her imagination ran rampant, imagining Case's big, tanned body sprawled against those whisper-soft sheets.

She swallowed hard, feeling the unmistakable rush of sexual arousal. This was bad. Very bad. Not only was she too busy for any kind of relationship, sexual or otherwise… but Case was one of Royal's most eligible bachelors. He wasn't likely to be interested in the hired help.

Mellie's family went way back in Royal, maybe as far back as Case's did. Despite that, when she eventually married and started a family, she wanted an ordinary man, one who would have time to be a daddy…a man who was interested in home and hearth.

As far as she could tell, Case had tried marriage and found it lacking. He'd be unlikely to dip his toes into that water again anytime soon, if ever. And since she wasn't the kind of woman who was comfortable having casual sex, there was no point in seeing Case Baxter as anything other than a paycheck and a valuable advertisement for Keep N Clean.

Feeling unaccountably morose, she told herself she was just tired after a long day's work. She gathered her things, let herself out and carefully locked the front door.

After the short drive back to town and a forty-five-minute stop at her office to check mail and phone messages that hadn't been routed to her personal cell, she headed for home. She had a date tonight with a favorite TV show, some leftover spaghetti and her comfy sofa.

But the plan changed when she found her father camped out on her doorstep. It looked as if he had been sitting there for a while, because he had an empty beer bottle at either hip. His eyes were bloodshot. Though he stood when she

walked up the path to the small duplex she called home, he was unsteady on his feet.

"You changed your locks," he said, a look of bafflement on his florid face. Harold Winslow was short and round with salt-and-pepper hair and skin weathered by the Texas sun. Once upon a time he had been a successful businessman. But when his beloved wife died, his alcoholic tendencies had taken over.

Hugging him briefly, she sighed. "I'm a grown woman, Daddy. I like my privacy. You don't seem to understand that." She had tried her best not to fall into a codependent relationship with her only living parent. But that was easier said than done.

The trouble was, Mellie felt his pain. Ila Winslow had been the center of their lives. When cancer took her away from her husband and sixteen-year-old daughter, their world had caved in. Harold found solace in whiskey. Mellie had been forced to grow up far too quickly.

Harold followed her into the house. "Any chance you might fix dinner for your dear old dad?"

She counted to ten beneath her breath, keeping her back to him. "We can order a pizza. I'm beat. I was planning to eat leftovers."

"Pizza works. You got any cash? I left my billfold at home."

It was an old game they played. Harold could live comfortably off the rents from the properties he still owned. But money slipped through his fingers like water through a sieve. When he ended up broke again and again, he came knocking at Mellie's door…sometimes figuratively, but more often than not, literally…like tonight.

Swallowing her disappointment at having her hopes for a peaceful evening shattered, she managed an even

tone. "Go ahead and order what you want. I'm going to change clothes."

By the time she returned to the living room, her father was sprawled in a recliner, the television remote in his hand. He gave her a smile, but behind it she thought she saw despair. His existence was aimless. No matter how hard Mellie tried, she couldn't get him to understand that his life wasn't over. She loved her dad, but once in a while, it would have been nice to lean on him instead of always having to be the grown-up.

Dinner arrived soon after. She paid for the two small, fragrant pizzas and tipped the young man, wondering if the fact that she and her father couldn't even agree on toppings was proof that she would never convince him to see things her way.

They ate in silence, the television filling the void. Finally, she finished her meal and decided it was now or never…a conversation that was long overdue. But she would come at it indirectly.

"I started a new job today, Daddy. I'm going to be cleaning and organizing for Case Baxter."

Harold raised an eyebrow. "The new Texas Cattleman's Club president?"

"Yes. Having him as a client will be a coup, I think."

"I'm proud of you, baby girl."

For once, she thought he meant it. "Thank you." She paused and said a prayer. "I'm doing well, Daddy. Keep N Clean is solvent and growing."

He nodded. "Good for you."

An awkward silence descended, but she forged ahead. "We need to talk about last week."

Immediately, his face closed up. "I'm fine," he muttered. "Quit worrying. I don't drink as much as you think I do."

"Sheriff Battle found you passed out in the street." She

hesitated, dreading his reaction. "I'd like to pay for you to go to rehab before it's too late."

"I hadn't eaten breakfast. My blood sugar was too low. I fainted, that's all."

"Daddy, please. I know you miss Mom. So do I. Every day. But at the rate you're going, I'm likely to lose you, too."

Harold lumbered to his feet and stood with what dignity he could. "There's nothing wrong with me. Surely a man can enjoy a couple of beers without getting a lecture."

It was more than beer. A lot more. And the alcohol abuse was aging him rapidly. "Just think about it," she pleaded. "It won't be so bad. I've read about some beautiful places right here in Texas. I want you to be healthy and strong so you can play with your grandchildren one day."

Her father snorted. "You don't even date. That cleaning company of yours won't keep you warm at night. Maybe you'd better quit worrying about me and find yourself a man."

It was exactly like Harold to go on the attack when she tried to talk to him about his drinking. "I've got plenty of time for that."

For a split second the naked pain in her father's heart was written on his face. "We all think we have plenty of time, Mellie. But love isn't a permanent gift. Losing it hurts. I'm pretty sure that's why you don't let any man get too close. I'll make you a deal, darlin'... When you get your life in order, I'll let you muck around with mine."

She stood at the door and watched him go...his gait slow but relatively steady. He'd had his driver's license revoked time and again. Fortunately, the home where Mellie had grown up and where Harold still lived was centrally located in Royal, making it possible for her father to walk to his destinations for the most part.

As she showered and got ready for bed, she pondered her father's words. It was true that she rarely went out on a date. She'd told herself that getting a business off the ground required determination and hard work. But did it demand the sacrifice of any kind of personal life?

Her pride stung a bit to know that her father had pegged her so well. In her desperate need to get him to admit his failings and seek help, had she overlooked her own response to grief?

Over the years, she hadn't cared enough for any of the men who populated her modest social life to let them get too close. Channeling her energy into Keep N Clean kept her focused. Romance would only get in the way of her life plan.

Ordinarily after a hard day, she was out by the time her head hit the pillow. Tonight, though, she couldn't get settled. Her father seemed increasingly out of control, and she didn't know what to do to help him. He was an adult…with resources. So why did she feel responsible for his actions?

Reaching for a more pleasant subject, she reminded herself that tomorrow she would have the opportunity to spend more time in Case Baxter's beautiful home. It had personality…and history. Bringing it to its full potential would be a pleasure. Not to mention the outside chance she might run into the man himself.

He'd given her a set of keys along with his permission to come and go as she liked during the day. According to Case, he was going to be very busy at the club and also with the ranch. She got the distinct impression he planned to make himself scarce as long as she was working in his house.

Something about that notion made her feel weird and discouraged. Case was exactly the kind of man she found appealing. It hurt that he wanted to avoid her.

Thumping her pillow with her fist, she rearranged the light blanket. The cold would come, but for now, her bedroom was stuffy.

She was finally almost asleep when her phone dinged quietly, signaling a text. Groaning, she reached for her cell and squinted at it in the dark.

Mellie—I hope I'm not disturbing you. I know it's late, but I wanted to tell you thanks. You're a miracle worker. I almost thought I was in the wrong house when I got home tonight. Kudos to Keep N Clean...

Case Baxter. The last person on earth she expected to be texting her at this hour, or any hour, for that matter. Was she supposed to answer? Or simply let him think she was asleep? She hesitated for a moment and then put down the phone.

It was nice of him to take the time to acknowledge her work. Perhaps the message was a peace offering after the argument that had started their day.

With a smile on her face, she snuggled back into the covers, unable to squelch the hope that she would run into Case tomorrow and maybe even see him in her dreams.

Four

Case jammed his Stetson as far down on his head as it would go and hunched his shoulders, trying to bury his chin in the collar of his rain jacket. The weather gods had finally sent Maverick County some moisture, but it wasn't the days-long, soaking rain they needed.

Instead, the precipitation was a miserable, icy-cold drizzle that chilled a man right down to the bone, a dramatic shift from the previous day. Since seven this morning, he'd been out riding the fence line with his foreman, looking for problems. They'd lost two dozen head of cattle in the past few weeks. Everyone suspected rustlers, but before Case involved the authorities, he wanted to make sure the animals hadn't simply wandered away through a hole in the fence.

Now, though he was wet and weary, at least he had the satisfaction of knowing that his fencing was not compromised. Giving the foreman a wave, Case turned his horse

and galloped back toward the house. Already this new housekeeper thing was getting in his way.

Ordinarily in a situation like this, he would strip down in the mudroom, walk through his house naked and climb into the hot tub on the sheltered back porch. Unfortunately, that wasn't going to happen today, with Mellie around.

Muttering beneath his breath, he handed off his horse to one of the stable guys in the barn and then strode toward the house. He was grumpy and wet and hungry, and he wanted his castle to himself. His bad mood lasted all the way up until the moment he found Mellie Winslow bending over the side of his bed dusting the base of one of the posts. She was wearing Spandex pants, the navy fabric curved snugly against a firm, shapely butt.

His heart lodged in his throat at about the same time his gut tightened with swift and wicked arousal that swept through his veins. He actually took half a step backward, because he was stunned.

Mellie straightened and smiled, her expression cautious. "Mr. Baxter. Case. I'm sorry. I didn't think you'd be home in the middle of the day. I can move on to another room for now."

He shrugged. "I need a hot shower. Won't be long." Unless maybe he got distracted imagining Mellie in there with him…

"I put fresh towels in your bathroom a few minutes ago. They're probably still warm from the dryer." She paused and seemed hesitant. "Have you had lunch?"

Come to think of it, he hadn't. Which might account for his surly attitude. "No. I'll grab something in a minute."

"Would you like me to fix soup and a sandwich? It's no problem."

His fingers were cold, his skin damp. But inside, he was

burning up. He should have hired a seventy-plus grand-motherly type with a bun and absolutely no sex appeal.

But he hadn't. Oh, no…not at all. He'd brought tempta-tion into his house. Hell, into his bedroom, to be exact. He cleared his throat. "That would be nice. Thanks."

Mellie nodded and walked away.

Case slumped against the wall, his heart thundering in his chest. There was far too much going on in his life right now to get sidetracked by a very inconvenient attrac-tion. He was a grown man. Not a boy. He could control his physical impulses.

In the shower he turned the water hot enough to sting his skin. Maybe the discomfort would take his mind off the fact that he had an erection…a big one. Damn. What was it about Mellie that caught him off guard and made him hungry to strip her naked and take her to bed?

She was beautiful in a girl-next-door kind of way, but Royal had more than its share of attractive women. Case didn't find himself panting after every one of them. Maybe it was the fact that Mellie was in his house.

That was *his* mistake.

He dried off and changed into clean clothes. His others, wet and muddy, lay in a pile on the bathroom floor. Pre-sumably, his new housekeeper would take care of wash-ing them.

Standing in the middle of his bedroom, he acknowl-edged the truth. He didn't *want* Mellie Winslow washing his clothes. He had far better plans for activities the two of them could enjoy.

It was bad enough that she was cleaning up after him. Maybe he was weird, or maybe his first marriage had ru-ined him, but he liked relating to women on an even foot-ing. Mellie was talented and capable and she was doing

exactly what he had hired her to do. So why was he getting freaked out about everything?

He found her in the kitchen. She hummed as she moved around the room. His oak table, situated in the breakfast nook, was set with a single place mat, a lone plate and glass and a set of silverware.

Mellie waved a hand. "It's all ready, if you want to sit down."

He leaned against the doorframe. "Aren't you joining me?"

Her eyes widened momentarily and a faint pink crept up her neck. "I had a big breakfast. I usually work through lunch."

"At least a cup of coffee, then. You're on the clock, and it's my clock." He smiled to put her at ease, since she was eyeing him dubiously.

"Okay."

He refused to sit at the table and be served as if he were in a restaurant. Instead, he waited until she placed the bowl of tomato soup and the grilled cheese sandwich at his place. "This looks great," he said. "Thank you."

"Coffee to drink?"

"Yes, please. Black."

Mellie poured two cups, added milk and sugar to hers, and then joined him as they both sat down. He hadn't realized how hungry he was until the aroma of freshly prepared food reached him and his stomach growled loudly.

It was Mellie's turn to grin.

They sat in companionable silence for a few moments, Mellie sipping her coffee and Case wolfing down the food she had prepared for him. Though soup and a sandwich wasn't exactly haute cuisine, the comfort food was filling and delicious.

"So tell me, Mellie…what are your ambitions for Keep N Clean?"

If she was surprised by his interest, she didn't show it. "When I'm dreaming big," she said, "I think about franchising and moving into medium-size towns all over Texas."

He raised an eyebrow. "I'm impressed. You must have a knack for numbers."

"I have an associate business degree. But most of the hands-on stuff is self-taught. It's important to discern what a client wants and then be able to provide it. Especially in a service industry like mine. You have to stand out from the pack."

"Very true, I'm sure." He finished his meal and stood to get more coffee. He held out the coffeepot. "More for you?"

Mellie shook her head. "No, thanks. I'd better get back to work."

"Not so fast," he said. The urge to detain her was unsettling. He had plenty to keep him busy. But he didn't want to walk away from Mellie. "Tell me about yourself."

Mellie smiled wryly. "Is that really necessary?"

"Humor me."

"Well…"

He watched her search for words and wondered if she was going to avoid any mention of her father. Fortunately, he was a patient man…so he waited.

She shrugged. "It's not very exciting. I grew up in Royal. My mom died of cancer when I was sixteen. My dad went into a tailspin of grief, meaning I ended up being the parent in our relationship. I knew I wanted to start my own business, so I looked around and tried to find something that filled a niche. Royal had an industrial cleaning company but nothing smaller, other than individuals who worked for themselves."

"And here you are."

She wrinkled her nose. "Working for the brand-new president of the Texas Cattleman's Club."

"Are all your employees as eye-catching in that uniform as you are?"

Her jaw dropped a centimeter. "Um..."

"Sorry. Was that out of line?"

"More like unexpected." She stared at him, gaze narrowed, clearly trying to get inside his head. "Someone told me that you don't like women invading your house."

He winced. Royal's gossipy grapevine was alive and well. "That's not exactly accurate."

"No?" She cocked her head as if to say she knew he was skirting the truth.

"I like my privacy. But since I have neither the time nor the inclination to round up dust bunnies or clean out the fridge, I have to make compromises."

"Ah."

"What does that mean?"

"It means I'm accustomed to wealthy people who barely even acknowledge the presence of a service worker. We're invisible to them. Nonentities."

He frowned. "I can't speak for all the comfortably well-to-do families in Royal, but my friends aren't like that."

"If you say so. And for the record, Case, no one would describe you as only 'comfortably well-to-do.'"

Mellie Winslow had a bit of a chip on her shoulder. He hadn't noticed it before, but she wasn't trying to hide it now. "Does my lifestyle offend you, Mellie?" he asked gently, wondering if she would rise to the bait.

She sat back in her chair, pushing a few stray wisps of hair from her forehead. The set of her jaw was mutinous. "Let's just say that I don't have a single Modigliani hanging in my hallway."

"My parents were art collectors. They traveled the world. But believe me when I tell you I would trade every sculpture and painting in this house to have Mom and Dad back with me for just one day."

Mellie knew she had stepped in it...big-time. She felt hot color roll from her throat to her forehead. The taste of shame was unpleasant. "I am *so* sorry, Case. You're right, of course. Relationships matter more than things. Money doesn't buy happiness."

He grinned at her, his scruffy chin making him dangerously attractive. His hair was still damp from his shower. "Don't get carried away. Money is good for a lot of things."

"Such as?"

He leaned his chair back on two legs, defying gravity, and crossed his arms over his chest. "Flying to Paris for the weekend. Buying a yacht. Scoring Super Bowl tickets. Supporting a charity. Spoiling a woman."

She had a feeling he threw that last one in to get a reaction.

There *was* a reaction. But it happened someplace he couldn't actually see. She cleared her throat. "Being spoiled is nice, but most women I know want to take care of themselves."

For the first time, she saw a shadow of cynicism on his face. "Maybe you know the wrong rich people and I know the wrong women."

Mellie stood abruptly, feeling out of her depth and alarmingly sympathetic toward the man who'd been born and reared with every possible advantage. "There's more soup on the stove, if you're still hungry. I really do have to get busy."

Case unfolded that long, lean body of his from the chair and joined her at the dishwasher, his hands brushing hers

as he put his plate alongside her cup. She felt his breath on her cheek when he spoke. "Is your boss such a slave driver?" he muttered.

She turned around to face him. They were almost in an embrace, the counter at her back and one big contrary cowboy planted in front of her. She lifted her chin and propped her hands behind her. "*I'm* the boss, Case. And I don't need to be spoiled. If I want to fly to Paris this weekend, I'll buy my own ticket."

His gaze settled on her lips. For one heart-thumping second, she knew he was going to kiss her. "Don't be so touchy, Mellie. There's nothing wrong with a man doing nice things for a woman."

Things? Oh, Lordy. "Um, no… I guess not." She stopped and looked him straight in the eyes. "Are you flirting with me, Case Baxter?"

He shrugged, a half smile doing interesting things to that enticing mouth. "What happens if I say yes?" His thick eyelashes settled at half-mast. She could smell the soap from his shower and his warm skin.

Her inclination was to tell him. The truth. The shivery, weak-in-the-knees truth. She wanted hot, sweaty, no-holds-barred sex with Case Baxter on his newly made bed.

But sadly, she was known for being smart and responsible. "I suppose if you say yes, I'll have to point out unpleasant things like sexual harassment in the workplace."

"You just told me I'm not your boss. We're here as equals, Mellie. So I guess whatever happens, happens."

Before she could react, he brushed his lips against her forehead, turned on his heel and strode out of the kitchen.

Mellie put her fingers to her lips like a schoolgirl who had just been kissed by the captain of the football team. Case's chaste kiss had not made contact with her mouth

at all. But she felt the imprint of his personality all the way to her toes.

Moving cautiously toward the window, she peeked out and saw him striding toward the barn. She hadn't expected him to actually *work* on his ranch. Which made no sense, because if Case had been an entitled, supercilious rich jerk, he'd never have been elected president of the Texas Cattleman's Club. People liked him.

She might like him, too, if she could get past the huge neon sign in her brain that said Off-Limits.

In the meantime, she had things to do and places to be.

The master suite had occupied most of her time today, and not only because she was fascinated with its owner. The bathroom and bedroom were huge. By the time three o'clock rolled around, she had deep-cleaned everything from the grout between the tiles to the wooden slatted venetian blinds.

In addition to an enormous teak armoire, the quarters boasted a roomy walk-in closet. Her fingers itched to tackle the chaos there, but that chore would require a chunk of time, so she would postpone it until tomorrow. No sense in starting something she couldn't finish.

She left earlier than the day before and told herself it wasn't because she was avoiding Case. He was an important client, true, but she still had to run her business.

Back at her office, she popped the top off a bottle of Coke and downed it with a sigh of pleasure. Sure, the sugar and caffeine weren't good for her, but as addictions went, the soda was fairly harmless.

Which was more than could be said for her inability to erase Case from her thoughts. If he was seriously testing the waters with her, she would have more to worry about than a sugar rush. Allowing herself to be lured into a multi-millionaire's bed would be the height of folly.

She knew herself pretty well. Guarded. Suspicious. Independent.

On the flip side, she was hardworking, generous and ambitious. The one thing that she was *not* was a good judge of men's motives. Perhaps because her mother had not been around to share advice, Mellie's father had gone overboard in warning her about guys and sex.

He'd told her sex was all boys wanted from a girl…that it was up to her to make good decisions. Well, here she was. Almost thirty. A modest financial success. A dutiful daughter. And only steps away from missing out on things like romance and motherhood and the chance to meet a man who could make her toes curl with his kisses.

Case might not be her idea of the perfect man for the long haul, but he might be exactly the right guy for the here and now.

Five

Case returned to the house at four thirty, anticipating another round of verbal sparring with the delightfully prickly Mellie. But her car was gone. Was she avoiding him? And didn't she know that the male of the species enjoyed a chase?

He had dinner plans with Nathan Battle tonight. Amanda was out for the evening with her book club. So Case and the sheriff were looking forward to medium-rare steaks, a couple of games of pool and a sampling of sports on Nathan's brand-new big-screen TV.

Nathan had offered to do the cooking. Case brought a case of imported beer and an apple pie he'd picked up at the bakery. The rain had ended several hours ago, so the two men sat outside in the gathering gloom and enjoyed the crisp air.

The scent of beef cooking made Case's stomach growl. Which made him think of the last meal he'd eaten. The

one a certain redhead with kind eyes and a stubborn chin had made for him.

Nathan kicked the leg of Case's chair. "I'm the quiet one. You're supposed to entertain me with tales of the rich and famous."

Case slunk farther down in his chair. "I'm not famous."

Nathan laughed out loud. "What's eating you, Baxter? I've had livelier conversations at a morgue. Is the new job title weighing you down?"

"I'm not official for ten more days, so no."

"Then what?"

Case drained his beer and popped the top on a second. "You're imagining things."

Nathan stood, flipped the steaks and sat back down with a sigh. "Then it must be the new housekeeper. Is she making you take off your shoes at the door? Or forbidding you to eat popcorn in the den?"

"Very funny. It's my house. I can do whatever the hell I please. Mellie doesn't run my life."

"Mellie? Wow. First names already?"

"I wasn't going to make her call me Mr. Baxter."

"Fair enough." The other man paused. "Here's the thing, buddy. I have to pass along a warning."

"A warning?"

"Yes. From Amanda. But to be honest, I agree with her."

"Should I be worried?"

"It's not a joke, Case. If you screw around with Mellie Winslow either literally or figuratively, Amanda will come after you. And my wife can be pretty scary when she's on her high horse."

"I don't understand."

"Mellie hasn't had an easy life. You're way out of her league."

"Now, wait a minute." Case felt his temper rise.

"I'm not insulting Mellie. She's great. But you're older than she is, more experienced, and your financial position puts you at an advantage. I'm merely suggesting you not do something you'll regret. I know you, Case. You're not interested in a serious commitment. Admit it."

Case dropped his head against the back of his chair, scowling at the crescent moon above. "You know what it's like to have a failed relationship in your past." Nathan and Amanda had spent years apart. They had been high school sweethearts, but malicious lies had destroyed that bond, and it had been a very long time before they'd reconnected.

"I do. It makes you second-guess yourself. Especially when the reason it happened was that you were young and stupid."

"Are we talking about me or you?"

"Both of us."

Fortunately, Nathan dropped the subject. The steaks were ready, and neither man was the type to spill his guts, even to a friend.

The rest of the evening was lighthearted and comfortable. Sports talk. Good food. But as Case drove back to the ranch later that night, disappointment filled his chest. Mostly because he knew the sheriff was right about Mellie.

She was not the type of woman to indulge in casual sex. And Case wasn't interested in anything else.

Mellie sat at her desk and groaned as she hung up the phone. Two of her employees had called in because their kids had the flu. Which meant a major juggling act on the boss's end. Several houses couldn't be postponed for one reason or another. She called a few clients who weren't tied to a certain schedule and changed their cleaning days, offering a credit toward next month's bill for the kerfuffle.

In half an hour, she had reassigned her workforce and

come to the inescapable realization that she was going to have to put Case off for a couple of days. It wasn't a problem in the grand scheme of things. He didn't have any big social events at his home coming up. He merely wanted her to deep-clean and organize his house.

Postponing the job for forty-eight or even seventy-two hours was not a crisis. But what made her squirm was the fact that Case Baxter would think she was running scared.

She was not completely inexperienced. There had been two serious relationships in her life, both of which she'd thought might turn out to be the real deal. But in the end, the first one had been puppy love, and the second a crush on a man fifteen years her senior.

When she'd finally realized that the older guy was more of a parental figure than a soul mate, she'd broken things off. That was four years ago. She'd been alone ever since. By choice.

She knew when a man wanted her. And she had the confidence to turn a guy down without apology. Her body was hers to give. She was old enough now to understand that true love was rare. Even so, she would not allow herself to be physically intimate with a man on a whim.

Case Baxter tempted her. Her own yearning was what scared her. She liked him and respected him. Even worse, no woman under eighty and in her right mind could be immune to his bold sex appeal.

He was at the height of his physical maturity. Tough, seasoned, completely capable of protecting a woman or giving her pleasure. He was wealthy, classy and intelligent.

Damn it. She was vulnerable around him, and the feeling, although stimulating, was not one she welcomed.

She didn't believe in postponing unpleasant tasks. Pulling out her smartphone, she rapidly composed a text...

Case—I have a couple of employees out today, so I have to cover some shifts. I'll be back at your place in a few days. Will give U a heads-up beforehand. Sorry for the inconvenience. Mellie Winslow

She added her name at the end because she wasn't sure he had entered her contact info into his phone. Before she hit Send, she stared at the words. She was shooting for businesslike and professional.

Would he read her message in that vein, or was her genuine need to postpone the Baxter house going to be seen as a ploy to snag his attention? Oh, good grief. The man probably didn't give a flip about whether or not his cleaning lady showed up. He probably flirted automatically.

She was making a mountain out of a molehill.

The next three days were long and physically taxing. Mellie worked hard, much as she had in the beginning. In her early twenties, by the sweat of her brow, she had turned Keep N Clean into a viable operation. Clearly, she needed to rethink her staffing situation, though. She couldn't continue to work on a shoestring.

She needed enough flexibility to handle unexpected illness on the part of her employees as well as the occasional new customer like Case. The past two weeks were a wake-up call. If she really had dreams for expansion, she would have to take her game up a notch.

The one thing that needled her now was Case's total lack of communication. Given his past behavior, she'd expected some kind of cheeky text from him in return. All she'd gotten was No problem, and that was it. Even this morning when she had messaged him to say she was returning to the B Hive Ranch, there had been no response.

Was he miffed with her for putting him off? Did he

think a man in his position deserved to be kept at the top of the list? Maybe it wasn't egalitarian, but the truth was, he did. The significant fee he was paying her, combined with the cachet of having him on her client list, made keeping Case happy a priority.

It was barely nine when she arrived at the ranch. She saw some activity out in the fields and down at the barn, but the house looked much as it always did. Case had probably been up at first light doing whatever he did when he wasn't tormenting unsuspecting housekeepers.

Though she would have died before admitting it, her heart beat faster than normal as she ascended the front steps. Another weather front had moved in. The morning air was damp and cold, reminding her that Thanksgiving was not far off on the horizon. The date fell early this year.

Hesitating at the front door, she held her key in her hand. Case still hadn't replied to her text saying she was on the way. But he hadn't said *not* to come.

What if he was in bed with a woman? What if he hadn't seen or heard her text? To stumble upon her client in a very personal moment would be humiliating in the extreme.

Muttering beneath her breath, she closed her eyes and wrinkled her nose, berating herself silently for having such a ridiculously over-the-top imagination.

At last, she knocked firmly, listened and finally opened the door. The house seemed empty. Besides, she'd heard the rumors about Case's famous rules. He didn't entertain females at his place.

After hovering in the foyer for several moments, she told herself she was being foolish. Today she was going to tackle Case's kitchen. The sooner she started, the sooner she could escape, and maybe she wouldn't have to deal with the aggravating rancher.

The house was cold, but she didn't adjust the heat. By

the time she'd been working for an hour she would be plenty warm. The windows in the yellow-toned kitchen were designed to let in lots of light, creating a cheery center to the house. But today the skies over Royal were gray and sullen.

November could go either way in Maverick County. At the moment, the weather was depressing and chilly to the bone.

Mellie left her jacket on, shivering in spite of herself. Her usual routine was to clean from the top down. Which meant unloading all the cabinets above the beautiful amber-toned granite countertop. In the utility cabinet she found a stepladder that was just tall enough to give her access all the way to the ceiling.

Cleaning the tops and outer surfaces of the cabinets was not so hard. But when she opened the first one, she grimaced. Dishes and other items were crammed in with no regard for maximizing space. There wasn't even the barest nod toward order.

The best thing would be to empty everything and then come up with a system for replacing items in a manner that would make them easy for anyone to find. The contents of the first couple of cabinets were puzzling. On the very top shelves she found exquisite antique china…lots of it, cream-colored with an intricate pattern of yellow and gold. Farther down were ultramodern dishes in black and white.

She frowned. She was no designer, but the monochrome set looked as if it belonged in a high-end loft in SoHo, not a historic ranch house in Texas. Maybe Case thought the old stuff was not masculine enough for his taste. That was a shame, because there was a good possibility that the stacks of delicate porcelain were something that had been handed down through his family for generations.

Glassware was heavy. By the time she had emptied three

cabinets—three shelves each—her back was aching. The little bottle of ibuprofen she kept in her purse was empty, but she remembered seeing some in Case's bathroom.

In the elegant hallway with its hardwood floor and celadon walls, she stopped dead when she heard a sound. A groan. Not the house creaking as old houses often did, but something human.

She hurried her steps. "Mr. Baxter... Case?"

Another sound, this one muffled.

By the time she reached the open doorway to Case's bedroom, she half expected to find him passed out on the floor, felled by a blow from a burglar. Her imagination ran rampant.

But the truth was equally distressing. Case lay facedown on his bed, wearing nothing except a white buttondown shirt and gray boxer briefs.

Thank goodness he was facedown. Her first response was honest and self-revelatory but not pertinent to the situation.

Was he drunk? Surely not on a weekday before noon. She said his name again, approaching the bed with all the caution of a zookeeper entering the cage of a sleeping lion.

When she was close enough to touch him, her brain processed the available info. His head was turned toward her, his face flushed with color. Thick eyelashes lay against his cheeks. His lips were parted, his breathing harsh.

Ever so gently, she laid her hand against his forehead. The man was burning up with fever. Case Baxter had the flu. Or at least something equally serious.

He moaned again as she touched him. When he turned on his side toward her, she stroked his hair before she realized what she was doing. It was the same caress she would have used with a hurting child.

But Case was no child. His big masculine body shook

uncontrollably, though his tanned chest was sheened with sweat. She probably shouldn't have noticed his chest, but with his shirt completely unbuttoned, his flat belly and the dusting of dark hair at his midriff were hard to miss.

Her knees were less than steady, and she felt a bit woozy. Even passed out cold, Case did something to her. Something not entirely comfortable.

Ignoring her inappropriate reactions to the half-naked man, she pushed and pulled at him until she had him covered all the way to the neck. Case's limbs were deadweight. The rest of him was equally heavy.

She sat down at the edge of the bed. On top of the covers. "Case?" she said. "Can you hear me?"

He muttered and stirred restlessly.

"Case." She put a hand on his shoulder, injecting a note of authority, hoping to pierce the layers of illness that shrouded him.

His eyelids fluttered. "What?" The word was slurred.

How long had he been like this? People *died* from the flu. Not that Case was elderly or an infant, but still. "You need a doctor," she said firmly. "Who can I call?"

The patient scrunched up his face. "Head hurts."

Those two words destroyed her defenses entirely. Her newest client might be handsome and rich and arrogant as heck, but right now he was just a man in need of help. "I'll get you some medicine," she said. "But I need to check with your doctor."

"Call Parker." The command was almost inaudible.

She knew who he meant. Parker Reese was a gifted doctor who had saved more than one newborn at Royal Memorial Hospital. Parker and Case were friends. But for the flu?

"Don't you have a regular doctor?"

"Call Parker…"

This time she could barely hear the words. "Sure," she

groused. "I'll call a very busy specialist in the middle of the day to talk about a case of the flu." But she didn't really have much choice. Picking up Case's phone from the bedside table, she sighed when she realized she couldn't access his contacts.

She shook his shoulder again. "I need your code, Case."

"2…2…2…2."

Was he delirious, or did he really have such a ridiculously easy password? Apparently the latter, because it worked. Seconds later she located Parker Reese's info and hit the green button.

She fully expected to get an answering machine, but on the third ring, a deep masculine voice answered. "Hey, Case. I'm about to go into surgery. What's up?"

Mellie flushed. Luckily, the highly educated doctor couldn't see her face. "Dr. Reese, this is Mellie Winslow. I showed up at Case Baxter's house this morning to clean and found him passed out on the bed. I think it's the flu, but I have no idea how long he's been like this."

"Several of us played poker last night. Case left early. Must have been feeling bad. I have a full schedule today, but I'll pop by this evening."

"And in the meantime?"

"Push fluids. Alternate acetaminophen and ibuprofen every two hours. Chicken soup and anything else bland."

"I don't think he's going to be eating anytime soon, but I'll try."

Parker's voice changed. "Do you want me to send out a nurse?"

Mellie hesitated. Two seconds. Three at the most. "Thank you, but no. I can do my work and look in on him from time to time. I don't think he would be happy if we brought a stranger in to look after him."

"Good point."

"I'm sorry I bothered you."

"No worries. I'm glad you did. I'll be by later to check on you both."

Mellie ended the call and stared at the man in the bed. Somehow she had gone from being a paid housekeeper to a volunteer nurse.

What would Case Baxter think of this new development?

Six

Mellie located both medicines and fetched orange juice from the kitchen, as well as a notepad to record the time. She didn't want to be responsible for overmedicating her patient. With a little prayer for patience, she returned to the bedroom.

It was a relief to know that Case hadn't been lying sick and alone in this big house for three days. But that also meant he still had tough hours ahead of him. The flu had hit early this year and with a vengeance. Many people had been caught off guard, thinking they still had time to get a flu shot. Fortunately, Mellie had already gotten hers.

Now she knew why Case hadn't answered her text this morning. He'd been out cold, maybe since he'd stumbled home last night. Poor man. She sat on the edge of the bed again, choosing to ignore the fact that the *poor* man was worth seven or eight figures. Even so, he was human. And at the moment he needed her.

She put a straw in the juice since she wasn't sure she

could coax him into sitting up. "Case…" She spoke in a loud voice, hoping to rouse him. He stirred but didn't open his eyes.

"Case." She touched his arm. While she'd been in the kitchen, he had tossed back the covers. His body was still hidden from the waist down, but a broad masculine chest was on display.

His skin was hot. Too hot. She said his name a third time. Finally, he lifted one eyelid. "Leave me alone."

Grumpy and sick was better than semiconscious. "Dr. Reese—Parker—said you need to drink some juice and take something for your fever."

Case rolled to his side, taking the covers with him. He started shivering again. Big, visible tremors that shook the bed. "Parker c-c-can kiss my a-a-ass."

Exasperated, she glared at the lump of truculent male. "You told me to call him."

"Did not."

"Oh, for goodness' sake." She moved around to the other side of the bed and crouched so she could reach his mouth with the straw. "Drink this. Now." She was only slightly astonished when he opened his lips and sucked down a good portion of the OJ.

The muscles in his throat worked. "Tastes good."

"Of course it does. Now open up one more time. You have to swallow these pills."

She tapped his chin. He cooperated, downing the medicine without protest, but afterward he blinked and focused his fever-glazed eyes on Mellie. "Did you just poison me?" he asked.

"Don't tempt me." She glanced at the clock. Hopefully, his temperature would improve in half an hour or so. She grabbed the extra blanket from the foot of the bed and spread it over Case. "Better?"

His nod was barely perceptible. "Thank you."

Those two words went a long way. He might be sick and ornery, but at least he had enough sense not to alienate the only person helping him. "I'll check on you again in a bit. Sleep, Case. That's all you need to do."

Unexpectedly, he reared up in the bed. "Gotta go to the bathroom." He lurched to his feet before she could stop him. And promptly fell over like a giant redwood. His head caught the edge of the bedside table as he went down. A trickle of blood oozed from the small wound.

Dear God in heaven. Save me from stubborn men. She got down on her knees beside him. "Are you okay?"

He rolled to his back, his face ashen. "I never get sick," he said, a look of puzzlement creasing his brow.

His bafflement would have been funny in another situation. But their predicament erased any humor she felt. How in the heck was she going to put him back in bed?

"Can you get on your hands and knees?" she asked. "I'll help you up."

"Of course I can." Five seconds passed. Then ten. Case didn't move. His eyes were half-open, his attention focused upward. "Please tell me there aren't really snakes on my ceiling."

"Your fever is very high. Those are swirly lines in the paint."

"Thank God." He closed his eyes, and his breathing became heavy.

Mellie rubbed his arm. "You said you needed to visit the bathroom. Let's go." Her heart contracted in sympathy, but she kept the drill-sergeant tone in her voice.

She pushed on his hip, hoping to give him a nudge in the right direction. Finally, muttering and coughing, he rolled over and struggled onto his knees.

"Good," she said. All men responded to praise, right?

Putting her arm around his shoulders, she urged him upward, her back screaming in protest. Fortunately, his brain got the message, and he finally stood all the way upright, albeit with a little stagger.

Slowly, carefully, she maneuvered him toward the open bathroom door. She had cleaned every inch of this luxurious space. It was now as familiar to her as her own. But somehow, with the master of the house sharing it with her, the area shrank.

Case noticed himself in the mirror. His mouth gaped. "I look like hell."

"No argument there." She steered him toward the commode.

Her patient locked his knees suddenly, nearly toppling both of them. "I don't need your help."

She counted to ten. "If you fall in here, you could kill yourself on the ceramic tile."

"I'll hold on to the counter."

"Fine." It wasn't as if she wanted to be privy to a personal moment, no pun intended.

Case leaned on the vanity. Mellie retreated and closed the door. She hovered in the middle of the bedroom, half expecting any minute to hear a crash. Instead, nothing but silence.

At last the commode flushed and water ran in the sink. Finally, she heard something she hadn't expected at all. "Mellie? I could use a hand."

She opened the door cautiously and found him sitting on a bench underneath the window. His face was pasty white. He looked miserable. The fact that he had actually asked for help spoke volumes.

Without comment, she leaned into him and looped her arm beneath his armpit and around his back. "You ready?"

He nodded. It was hard to keep a professional distance

from a guy when pressed hip to hip with his big, muscular body. Fortunately, the brief trip across the bedroom rug passed without incident. She managed with Case's help to get him underneath the covers and settled with his head on a pillow.

Without thinking, she put a palm to his forehead to gauge whether or not his temperature was improving. Though Case was clearly befuddled, he raised one eyelid. "You should go home."

His voice was hoarse and thready. She could barely make out the words. "I marked off my book today to work on your house. I'm cleaning the kitchen. It's no trouble to check on you now and then." It was possible he didn't even hear her response. Already his chest rose and fell with steady, harsh breathing.

There was nothing she could do for him now. Instead, she returned to the kitchen and tackled the mess she had made. She had learned a long time ago that to completely overhaul a closet or a cabinet meant creating chaos in the beginning.

The rest of the day crawled by. Dr. Reese's reference to bland foods was a moot point. It was all she could do to coax Case into drinking water and juice from time to time—that and keep him medicated.

At five o'clock she had a decision to make. She didn't have a child at home or a husband waiting. If she'd been in the middle of something jobwise, she would have stayed an extra half hour to complete the task.

But the kitchen was mostly finished, no mess in sight. And Case's request to put his house in order came with no timeline, no urgency. So there was no reason for her to hang around except for the fact that Case Baxter was sick and alone.

They barely knew each other...at least if you overlooked

the not-so-subtle physical attraction and the way he had almost kissed her earlier in the week. Still, this wasn't about flirting or finding a possible love interest or even indulging in some carnal hanky-panky.

Her current situation was dictated by the need of one human to help another.

Wow, even in her head that sounded like pretentious rationalization.

Finally, she worked out a compromise between her conscience and her sense of self-preservation. She would wait for Dr. Parker Reese to arrive, and then she would head home.

Seven o'clock came and went. Then eight. Then nine. The sun had long since set. Outside, the world was cold and gray. Case's house echoed with silence.

Mellie lived alone, and she was perfectly happy. Why was she so worried about a man who chose to be a bachelor? He liked his freedom and his privacy. It was only because he was sick that she felt sorry for him. Surely that was it.

At nine thirty Case's cell rang, with Parker Reese's number appearing on the caller ID. Mellie had kept Case's phone with hers, not wanting him to be disturbed.

She hit the button. "Hello? Mellie Winslow here."

Parker sounded harried and distracted. "I am so sorry, Ms. Winslow, but we've had two moms check into the hospital in early labor and they're having problems. I'll likely be here most of the night. How is Case?"

"He's sleeping. The fever is down some, but it hasn't broken." She'd found a thermometer in Case's bathroom and had kept tabs on the worrisome numbers.

"You're doing the right things. Don't hesitate to call or text if he seems dramatically worse."

"Oh, but I—"

Parker said something to someone in the background, unwittingly interrupting Mellie's response. "I've got to go," he said, his tone urgent. "Keep me posted."

Mellie hung up and stared at the phone. How had she gotten herself into such a predicament?

She wandered down the hallway and stood in the doorway of Case's bedroom, watching him sleep. Today was Friday. The only things she had planned for the weekend were laundry, paying bills and a movie with a girlfriend on Sunday afternoon. Nothing that couldn't be postponed.

But what would happen if she stayed here? Case might be furious.

Then again, could she live with herself if she went home and something happened to him? He was wretchedly sick, certainly not in any shape to prepare food or even to remember when he had taken his doses of medicine. As long as the fever remained high, he might even pass out again.

Her shoulders lifted and fell on a long sigh. She didn't really have much choice. Only a coldhearted person could walk out of this house and not look back. Even if Case hadn't been handsome and charming and sexier than a man had a right to be, she would have felt the same way.

It was no fun to be ill. Even less so for people who weren't married or otherwise attached. Fate and timing had placed her under the man's roof. She would play Clara Barton until he was back on his feet. When that happened, if he tossed her out on her ear, at least her conscience would be clear.

Her bones ached with exhaustion. Not only had she worked extremely hard today, she'd spent a lot of time and energy on her patient. Suddenly, a hot shower seemed like the most appealing thing in the world. Fortunately, she kept spare clothes in the car for times when she needed to change out of her uniform.

Though it seemed like the worst kind of trespassing, she made use of one of the guest bathrooms and prepared for bed. She found a hair dryer under the sink and a new toothbrush in the drawer. In less than twenty minutes, she had showered and changed into comfy yoga pants and a soft much-washed T-shirt.

Case's king bed was large and roomy, and he was passed out cold. She would get more rest there than if she slept in the guest room and had to be up and down all night checking on him.

That reasoning seemed entirely logical right up until the moment she walked into his bedroom and saw that he had, once again, thrown off the covers. The man might have the flu, but looking at him still made her pulse race.

She would have to set the alarm on her phone for regular intervals, because Case was still racked with fever. When she managed to get the thermometer under his tongue and keep it there for long enough to record a reading, it said 101.2 degrees. And that was with medication.

No telling how high it would go if left untreated.

She gave him one last dose of acetaminophen, coaxed him into drinking half a glass of water and straightened his covers. After turning on a light in the bathroom and leaving the door cracked, she stood by the bed.

When this was all over, he would be back to his bossy, impossible self. But for now, he was helpless as a baby.

Refusing to dwell on how unusual the situation was, she walked around to the other side of the bed and sat down carefully. Case was using two of the pillows, but she snagged the third one for herself. There was no way she was going to climb underneath the covers, so she had brought a light blanket from the other bedroom.

Curling into a comfortable position, she reached out and turned off the light.

* * *

Case frowned in his sleep. He'd been dreaming. A lot. Closer to nightmares, really. His head hurt like hell and every bone in his body ached. Not only that, but his mouth felt like sandpaper.

He had a vague memory of someone talking to him, but even those moments seemed unreal.

Suddenly, the shaking started again. He remembered this feeling…remembered fighting it and losing. Aw, hell…

He huddled and gritted his teeth.

Above his head, a voice—maybe an angel—muttered something.

He listened, focused on the soft, soothing sound. "Oh, damn. I didn't hear the alarm. Case, can you hear me? Hold on, Case."

Even in the midst of his semihallucinatory state, the feminine voice comforted him. "S'kay," he mumbled. "I'm fine."

Vaguely, he was aware of someone sticking something under his tongue, cursing quietly and making him drink and swallow. "You are definitely *not* fine."

The angel was upset. And it was his fault. "Hold me," he said. "I can't get warm. And close the windows, please."

The voice didn't respond. Too bad. He was probably going to die and he'd never know what she looked like. Angels were girls, weren't they? All pink and pretty with fluffy wings and red lips and curvy bodies…

Belatedly, he realized that if he survived whatever living hell had invaded his body, he might get struck dead for his sacrilegious imagination.

Suddenly, his whole world shifted from unmitigated suffering to *if this is a dream, I don't want to wake up.* A body—feminine, judging by the soft breasts pressed up

against his back—radiated warmth. He would have whimpered if it hadn't been unmanly. *Thank you, God.*

One slender arm curved around his waist. "You'll feel better in the morning, Case."

The angel said it, so it must be true. Doggedly, he concentrated on the feel of his bedmate. It helped keep the pain away. Soft fingers stroked his brow. Soft arms held him tight.

Maybe he would live after all.

Seven

Case opened one eyelid and groaned when a shard of sunlight pierced his skull. *Dear Jesus.* If this was a hangover, he was never going to drink again. And if this was hell, he was going to beg for another chance to relive his thirty-six years and hope for a better outcome.

He moved restlessly. Even his hair follicles hurt. His chest felt as if someone had deflated his lungs. But his brain was clearer than it had been. Though he didn't want to, he made himself open both eyes at the same time. Sitting in an armchair beside his bed was Parker Reese.

Parker hadn't yet noticed that Case was awake. The other man was checking emails and/or texts, frowning occasionally and clicking his responses.

Case cleared his throat. "Am I at death's door? Have you come to show me the error of my ways?"

His doctor friend sat up straight, his gaze sharpening as he turned toward the bed. "You should be so lucky. No...you're going to be fine." Even so, Parker's expres-

sion held enough concern to tell Case that something serious was afoot.

"I didn't know you made house calls." Turned out, it even hurt to talk.

"I don't. Here. Drink something." Parker picked up a glass of ice water and held the straw to Case's lips.

Case lifted his head and downed the liquid slowly, trying not to move more than necessary. "Seriously. Why are you here?"

Parker's eyes widened, expressing incredulity. "Maybe because you're half-dead with the flu?"

"Only half?" Case tried to joke, but it fell flat.

Parker pulled out his stethoscope, ignoring Case's wince when the cold metal touched his skin. Listening intently as he moved the disc from side to side, Parker frowned. "We have to watch out for secondary infections, pneumonia in particular."

"How did you know I was sick? Did I look that bad when I left the poker game last night?"

Parker sat back, his head cocked with a clinician's focus. "Today is Saturday. The poker game was Thursday night."

Case gaped at him. "What happened to Friday?"

This time Parker's grin held a note of mischief that rattled Case. "You tell me. I've only been here twenty minutes."

Case subsided into the warm nest of covers and searched his brain for an explanation. He remembered someone in the bed with him, but that someone definitely hadn't been male. He'd been far too sick for any fooling around, so the woman he remembered must have been a dream.

He wet his chapped lips with his tongue. "No more jokes, Parker. Did I really lose an entire day? Surely you didn't

wait on me hand and foot. You're a good friend, but not that good."

Parker chuckled. "I'll take pity on you. Yes, you lost a day. You've been out of it for thirty-six hours. And no. I wasn't here to help, though I'm damned sorry about that. You picked the worst possible time to get sick. We've had baby after baby born at the hospital, some of them in worse shape than you, unfortunately. I haven't even been to bed yet, but I wanted to see how you were doing."

"Then who—?"

Parker held up his hand. "Mellie Winslow showed up to work yesterday morning and found you semiconscious, burning up with fever. She stayed with you all day and all night. To be honest, you might have ended up in the hospital if it weren't for her. You've had it rough."

"Damn." It was the best response Case could summon, and the most articulate. With a sinking feeling in his stomach, he remembered someone helping him into and out of the bathroom. Mellie Winslow? Good Lord. "Where is she now?" he asked hoarsely.

"I sent her home so she could change clothes and get some rest."

"Is she coming back?"

"I'd say that's up to you. Mellie knows you like your privacy."

Case winced. "Yeah, I guess she does." He'd certainly hammered home that lesson when he hired her. "I don't know why she stayed with me. I haven't been exactly cordial." In fact, he'd been a bit of a jerk the last time he saw her.

Parker shrugged. "I can hang around until midday. That gives you some time to think it over."

By the time noon came and went, Case had managed a shower with only a little help, had consumed a modest

breakfast and lunch, and had realized with no small dose of humility that he had a lot for which to be thankful. Maybe he could salve his conscience concerning Parker by writing another large check to the hospital. Parker got absolutely giddy when he talked about upgrading technology in the NICU.

But what about Mellie?

Parker was on the way out the door when his phone dinged. Case saw his buddy glance down and then look at him.

"What?" Case asked. "Who is it?"

"Mellie wants to know if she needs to come back. What should I tell her?" There was no judgment in Parker's steady gaze.

"I barely know her," Case muttered. "She's not under any obligation to take care of me."

"She's a nice woman. You could do worse."

"Nathan says Amanda will hunt me down and neuter me if I trifle with her friend."

"Trifle?"

"You know. Play around with her."

Parker shook his head in disgust. "I *know* what the word means. Are you tempted to *trifle*?"

"I don't know. Maybe. She's seen me at my worst."

"Is that a good thing or a bad thing?"

"I'm pretty sure Mellie Winslow isn't interested in my money."

"We were talking about you and the flu. Have you changed the subject?"

Case leaned against the doorframe, his knees the consistency of spaghetti. "I need to get back in bed."

"Yes, you do. Your color is lousy."

"Tell her I'll call her after I take a nap."

"You sure?"

Case nodded. "Yeah. Maybe by then I'll have had an epiphany."

"Sounds painful."

"Very funny." Case held out his hand. "Thank you."

Parker returned the handshake. "Glad I could help. If you get worse, don't hesitate to call. Men make lousy patients. Being a hero in this situation is the worst thing you could do."

"Duly noted."

With Parker gone, the house was quiet again. Case stumbled back to his bedroom and fell facedown on the bed. Parker had made him swear to take medicine on schedule. Case intended to keep that promise, but first he had to sleep.

Mellie paced from one side of her smallish living room to the other. Dr. Reese had said that Case would be in touch. But Reese had contacted her right after lunch, and it was now almost five o'clock.

In the interim, she had put together a dish of homemade lasagna and baked that, along with some oatmeal cookies. The house smelled wonderful, but it looked as if she was going to be eating alone.

She could hardly expect Case to be grateful for her help. Men hated feeling vulnerable. Case probably loathed the realization that Mellie had played nurse. Besides, there was a chance he didn't even remember her being there.

But Mellie remembered. Wow, did she. In the middle of the night when Case had finally stopped shivering and his temperature had moderated, she had relaxed enough to doze with him in her arms. She didn't sleep deeply. But when she roused again and again to check on her patient's condition, it had been a shock to find herself entwined with him in a quasi-intimate position.

Gradually, as the night waned, she'd felt something shift inside her. No matter how much she wanted to maintain boundaries for her own emotional protection, after this weekend she would never be able to look at Case the same way again.

The fact that he hadn't called or even sent her a text this afternoon told her he wanted her to stay away. The loud silence hurt. Even though she thought she understood why he hadn't made contact, her feelings were bruised. In truth, she might have to assign someone else to continue cleaning Case's house. The situation was likely untenable.

Telling herself not to be maudlin and foolish, she wandered into the kitchen and found a paper plate and some plastic utensils. She was too tired to worry about cleaning up after herself, and since she had unloaded the dishwasher only an hour before, she didn't want to make a mess.

She was moments away from scooping out a small serving of pasta when her phone made a quiet noise. Her heart pounding, she wiped her hands and glanced at the screen.

Are you busy?

It was Case.

No. Are you hungry?

She told herself she was only being a Good Samaritan. That she wasn't throwing caution to the wind and launching herself willy-nilly into a situation that was wildly inappropriate. Feeding a neighbor in need was a Texas tradition.

Her phone buzzed again.

I'm starving.

I made lasagna. Would you like me to bring you some?

I don't want to interrupt your evening.

She smiled in spite of herself.

It's no trouble. See you soon.

Working rapidly, she covered the casserole dish and wrapped it in towels to keep it warm. The loaf of fresh bread from the bakery in town could be heated in Case's microwave. Even if Dr. Reese had provided lunch for his friend, that was a long time ago. She didn't want Case to wait any longer than necessary.

On the way out to the ranch, she lectured herself. *Stay calm. Don't let him bait you. Treat him like a brother.*

There were two problems with that last suggestion. Number one—she'd never had a brother. And number two—her reactions to Case Baxter bore no resemblance at all to sibling affection. He disturbed her, provoked her and made her want things.

Unfortunately, the trip was not long enough to gain any real handle on the situation. Before she knew it, she was unloading the car and making her way up the steps of Case's home. With her arms full, she had no choice but to ring the bell.

It was almost a full minute before the door opened. Case stood there staring at her, the planes of his face shadowed in the harsh glare of the porch light. "Please come in," he said.

In the foyer, he insisted on taking most of the load away from her. As she followed him to the kitchen, she couldn't help but notice the way his gray sweatpants rode low on his hips. In the midst of the cheery room she had worked

so hard to organize, the lighting was better. Now she could see all of Case. His navy cotton shirt was unbuttoned, revealing a white T-shirt underneath that clung to the contours of his muscled chest.

When she could tear her gaze away from all that male magnificence, she saw—as she'd suspected—that he was definitely not 100 percent. His eyes were sunken and his hair was askew. But he smiled.

"This smells amazing, Mellie."

"I hope you like Italian food. I suppose I should have asked about your preferences before I fixed something."

"I'm not a picky eater."

He set the containers on the table and pulled out her chair. "Let me get you a glass of wine," he said. But she noticed that despite his polite manners, he was weaving on his feet.

"Oh, for heaven's sake." She resisted his attempt to make her take a seat. His skin was clammy and his hands unsteady. "You look like you're about to pass out. Sit down, Case. Now."

Surprisingly, he obeyed, but said, "I don't expect you to wait on me." The statement was a shade on the belligerent side.

She handled him the same way she would a fractious toddler. "You're not well. Sit there and rest while I get things ready."

He didn't argue, but his gaze followed her as she moved around his kitchen. His eyes were dark, his unshaven jaw tight. "I owe you an apology," he said. "For what happened when you were here before."

She shot him a look. "You mean last night?"

His jaw dropped noticeably before he snapped it shut. Dark color slashed his cheekbones. "I don't remember much about last night."

For once, she had the upper hand. He was juggling a healthy dose of discomfiture. It was almost funny to see the suave, self-assured cowboy off his game. "Not much to remember." She set a plate of food in front of him. "Eat it before it gets cold."

He grabbed her wrist, not painfully, but firmly. Enough to stop her in her tracks. "I made inappropriate remarks about your clothing. I kissed you. I'm sorry."

Resting her hand on his shoulder, she let herself lean on him. "Don't be silly. You gave me a compliment. I was flattered. And the truth is, you're *not* my boss. You were right. We're equals. A man and a woman."

"And last night?"

When she slept in his bed, holding him in her arms? "Last night was nothing," she said. "You were sick. I couldn't very well leave you here alone. I'm glad you're on the mend."

When she sat down and took a bite of her lasagna, she almost choked at the look on Case's face. His laser stare made her squirm in her seat. There was no way he could know for sure. He'd been too feverish and addled to understand that she had held him like a lover, doing everything she could to give him comfort.

He finally picked up his fork, but he never took his eyes off her. "Parker told me I lost an entire day…that I had a very high fever. He said I might have ended up in the hospital if you hadn't been here to look after me."

"I think your friend exaggerates. It was no big deal."

Case leaned across the table and put his hand over hers. "It is to me. Thank you, Mellie. For everything."

Eight

Case knew he had shocked her. Hell, he had shocked himself. He wasn't a touchy-feely kind of guy. Beneath his hand, Mellie's fingers were soft and delicate. An impression at direct odds with what he knew to be the truth about the woman. She was strong and independent. She didn't need a man to take care of her. Which made it all the more inexplicable that he had the strongest urge to do that very thing.

He forced himself to release her. "Sorry," he muttered. "I didn't mean to make you uncomfortable." She had the look of a rabbit frozen in the grass, trying to appear invisible.

Mellie shook her head. "I'm not uncomfortable. But I'm trying to figure you out."

When he made himself take a bite, he realized how hungry he was. He chewed and swallowed, weighing her words. "I'm an open book."

She snorted and tried to cover it up as a cough. "Um, no."

"Explain yourself, woman." He waved a fork in the air. When Mellie smiled at him, he felt a tug of desire low in his belly.

"First of all," she said, "you're wealthy and available, but you don't date. At least not in Royal."

"How would you know that?" She had him spot-on, but that was beside the point.

"I have my sources." Now her smile was wry.

"Go on."

"You're a self-professed privacy junkie, but you know everyone in town, and you are so popular and well regarded the powers that be elected you president of the Cattleman's Club."

"Liking privacy is not necessarily the same as being a hermit."

"True."

He circled back to the most promising point. "I'm flattered that you've studied me."

Mellie shook her head. "Don't be. Your ego is too healthy as it is."

"Ouch." He paused, realizing that he was deliberately flirting with Mellie. But his sexual overture wasn't necessarily being reciprocated. "Ego is neither good nor bad. I think it's a matter of degree."

"And where would you fall on that scale? Somewhere near the top, I think."

He stared at her, no longer amused. "You might be surprised." Finishing his meal, he stood and poured himself another glass of wine, cursing the fact that his legs were wobbly. Sadly, it had nothing to do with the modest amount of alcohol he had consumed. How long was this damned flu going to keep him down? He had places to go, people to see.

At his best, he would have enjoyed sparring with Mellie

Winslow. But he was definitely not at his best. He brought the bottle with him to the table and collapsed into his chair, trying not to let on that he was light-headed.

Mellie studied him. "You need to be in bed," she said.

"Will you join me?" The words popped out of his mouth uncensored. His subconscious was an uncivilized beast.

His dinner companion gaped. Her mouth snapped shut as hot color reddened her cheeks. "What is it about men?" she muttered, the question apparently rhetorical.

Now he had her measure. If he wanted to keep Mellie off balance and not the other way around, all he had to do was give her the unvarnished truth about what he wanted from her. "What do you mean?"

She shrugged. "You're barely able to stand, and still you obsess about sex."

"It's in our DNA. We can't help it. Especially when a beautiful woman brings us dinner and plays nurse."

"I wasn't playing last night. You were sick."

"I'm only sorry I wasn't able to enjoy it."

"Case!"

Now it was out in the open. He wanted her. And he was almost certain she wanted him, too. But he needed confirmation before he went any further. He would never pursue a woman who wasn't interested.

"There's a strong spark between us. But tell me you don't feel it, and I'll leave you alone. Am I wrong?"

He saw the muscles in her throat work as she sputtered and looked anywhere but at him. "You're not wrong."

Three words. Three damn words, and he was hard as granite. He studied her, unable to come up with a response. She wasn't wearing her uniform. Instead, soft denim jeans outlined long legs and a narrow waist. In deference to the weather, she wore a pale green pullover sweater. The

V-neck exposed a long porcelain-skinned throat and fragile collarbone.

A man could get lost nibbling his way across that territory.

Under other circumstances, he would have stripped her naked and taken her on this kitchen table. Tonight, however, he had to accept his limitations. "Sadly, I don't have the stamina at the moment to follow up on that interesting admission."

"There's no reason you should." She appeared entirely, frustratingly calm...until one noticed the way her lips trembled the tiniest bit.

"We're dancing around this, aren't we?" The woman who almost certainly didn't have casual sex and the man who wanted more than he was able to give at the moment.

Mellie stood, resting her hands on the back of her chair. "I'll come back tomorrow...with more food."

"Don't be afraid of me, Mellie." He meant it. He couldn't bear the notion she might think he was blasé about this. The level of his fascination with her, the depth of his hunger, made no sense. But he wasn't a man to walk away from something he wanted. Even when having her and protecting her seemed to be two diametrically opposed behaviors.

And that wasn't even considering the fact that his actions might spark the wrath of Amanda Battle...or worse, her sheriff husband.

"I'm not afraid of you," Mellie said, her beautiful eyes grave. "Or even afraid of the possibility of us. But I've never started a physical relationship with a man, knowing up front that it had an expiration date."

Her words made sense. He even understood her caution. The feminine hesitation, though, only made his libido fight all the more to be heard. "It's not necessary to plan every turn in the road in advance...is it?"

Temper sparked in her expressive eyes. "Do me the favor of not pretending, Case. If I have sex with you, we both know it will be a physical thing only. No hearts and flowers. No pledges of undying love."

"That's pretty cynical."

"But accurate."

He wanted to argue, but he didn't have a leg to stand on. Mellie had pegged him pretty well. "So that's a no?" Never in a million years would he admit that her harsh assessment of his motives stung. Most women in this situation would be all over him.

But he was rapidly learning that Mellie Winslow was not *most* women.

She shrugged. "Let's take it a day at a time. This flu isn't going to go away overnight. Maybe you'll have the opportunity to rethink your invitation."

"Don't go," he said gruffly. He wanted her here…under his roof. In a way he hadn't wanted anything in a very long time. "It's not like I can seduce you. I can barely hold my head up."

Mellie shivered, though the kitchen was warm. He was doing it again. Winnowing away her good intentions. Trying to pretend that he wasn't the Big Bad Wolf and Mellie a wretchedly willing Red Riding Hood.

"I can't stay the night." That was a lie. She *could*. But she wouldn't.

"A movie, then. I'm sick of lying in bed."

"Such a touching offer. I'm better than boredom."

"You have a smart mouth."

She took pity on him. Beneath his masculine swagger, he was the color of milk. "I'll stay for a while."

"Good."

When he got to his feet, she moved closer and slipped

an arm around his waist, inhaling the smell of warm male. "I don't want to scrape you off the floor again."

He chuckled, the low sound making her catch her breath. "Is that how I got the knot on my skull?"

"Let's just say that you were not the best patient last night."

He kissed the top of her head casually, as if they were an old married couple wandering down the hall to watch a favorite TV program. "You're more than I deserve."

"Damn straight." Making Case Baxter laugh was fast becoming her life's work. But it was either that or give in to the urge to join the handsome, bad-to-the-bone cowboy in his bed.

They had their next argument in the den. Case collapsed on the expensive leather sofa and crooked an arrogant finger. "Come sit with me, Mellie."

"I'll be fine right here." She snagged a spot on the matching love seat, a safe distance away from the heavy-eyed male. "Have you taken your medicine?"

He scowled at her. "Is that all you can talk about? You're a broken record."

"I'll get it," she said wryly. Clearly, he was feeling like roadkill and didn't want to admit it.

When she returned after gathering what she needed from his bedroom and the bathroom, Case was holding the remote, his expression moody as he channel surfed. She put a hand on his forehead, not surprised to find it ferociously hot.

"Take these." She shook a couple of caplets into her palm and held out a glass of water.

"I feel fine."

His big body radiated tension. They had entered dangerous territory. Case was physically frustrated, not only from sexual arousal but because his brain was writing a

check his body couldn't cash. As far as she could tell, he was holding himself upright by sheer stubbornness.

She nudged his knee, keeping her tone light and gentle. "Be reasonable, and I'll sit with you. You can put your head in my lap."

It was the perfect opening for some of his sharp-edged sexual innuendo. The fact that he said nothing worried her. He must feel worse than she realized.

When he finished the glass of water—and in the process downed his meds—he stretched full-length on the sofa. Mellie sat down as promised, stroking the hair from his forehead. "Do you really want to watch a movie?" she asked.

He shook his head without opening his eyes. "No. I feel like hell."

"Okay, then…"

After a few seconds, Case's breathing deepened, and she knew he had fallen asleep. The old house creaked and popped as it settled for the night. On the mantel, a beautiful clock ticked away the minutes.

The moment was surreal. How had she and Case transcended so many social barriers so quickly? She was the hired help. He was the rich cowboy. He had one failed marriage behind him. She'd always been too afraid of loss to give marriage a try.

Yet here they were. As intimate together as if they had already become lovers.

With nothing else to command her attention, she traced the shell of his ear with her fingertip, trying to imagine what he would be like in bed. Healthy. Vigorous. Demanding.

She pressed her legs together, her insides shaking with what could only be described as lust. Delicious, quivery,

melting need. Heaven help her when Case was back to his old self.

Right now he was like some brilliant sun dimmed by a dust storm. The essence of the arrogant cowboy was still there but muted. The reduced kilowatts made it possible for her to keep up her guard. Maybe it was his vulnerability that stripped away her defenses and misgivings. Perhaps Case Baxter had seduced her without even trying.

The evening waned along with her need to hold him at bay. Would she end up sharing his bed? Why shouldn't she? Becoming Case's lover might well turn out to be the highlight of her adult life.

She knew most of the available men in Royal. Not one of them had sparked more than a fleeting interest in her over the years. So maybe she was destined to be happily single, a focused businesswoman, a dutiful daughter and a generous friend.

Living alone was not a dreadful thought. She understood Case in that respect. There was something to be said for peace and quiet and the chance to spend time with your thoughts. Case valued his privacy. Mellie valued her independence. It was a match made in heaven.

Temporary. Wildly enjoyable. Mutually satisfying.

Regretfully, the two of them were not going to get intimate tonight.

At nine o'clock she eased out from under her not-unwelcome burden and stood to stretch the kinks out of her muscles. Case never made a sound. He was deeply asleep.

His chin was shadowed with the beginnings of a dark beard. Even though she had seen him numerous times with his customary scruffy facial hair, now he looked far less civilized.

She felt guilty for leaving him like this. Still, he was a grown man and she was under no obligation, ethically

or otherwise, to stay. Parker Reese would check on him eventually.

After tidying the kitchen and gathering her things, she slipped out the front door and locked it behind her. Unfortunately, when she arrived at home, she found her father sitting on the doorstep again.

Nine

She greeted him with a grimace. "It's late, Dad. What do you want?"

He didn't even offer to help her carry anything into the house. Which, unfortunately, was typical. Harold Winslow spent most of his time worrying about Harold Winslow.

"I need to borrow fifty bucks, baby girl. Just until Monday. I'm good for it."

She'd long since given up keeping track of her father's IOUs. His requests were always modest amounts. Fifty here, a hundred there. Even when she gently reminded him he owed her money, he was all smiles and apologies. But the repayment never took place.

It was her own fault. All she had to do was cut him off, and he would get the message…eventually. But regardless of his failings, Harold was her father. He'd helped raise her, and he'd been the one she'd clung to when her mother died. He was her own flesh and blood.

"Why do you need the money, Daddy?" She dumped everything on the kitchen counter and confronted him.

Harold gaped, his expression both astonished and cagey. She'd never before pressed him about where the cash went. She hadn't wanted to know.

His bloodshot eyes stared back at her. "I had a lot of bills this month," he muttered.

"Is that why you don't have enough left for drinking tonight and tomorrow?"

"I don't appreciate your tone," he snapped.

She had definitely ruffled his feathers. But at the moment, she was so tired and dispirited she didn't care. "I'm not an ATM. I have expenses of my own and a business to support."

"Where have you been tonight?"

The change of topic caught her off guard. After a split second's hesitation, she saw no reason to dissemble. "I took dinner to Case Baxter. He has the flu."

"Well, ain't that sweet."

Her father's colloquial sarcasm nicked her patience. "I'm tired, Daddy. And it's late. Why don't you go home and have a rum and Coke…without the rum."

Harold's face turned red. "What's gotten into you, girl? If you think hangin' out with that fancy-ass richer-than-God cowboy makes you something special, you're wrong. Big-shot ranchers don't marry women who clean their toilets."

His deliberate crudeness broke her heart a little bit. Was this what they had come to? She refused him one time and he attacked?

Her chest aching with emotion, she reached for her purse, opened it and took out a handful of bills. When she held out her hand, Harold grabbed the money as if he was afraid she might change her mind.

Suddenly, her father was all smiles. "You're good to your old dad. I won't forget it." He folded the money clumsily and stuffed it in his shirt pocket.

She dug her teeth into her bottom lip, trying not to cry. "I'm done, Daddy. This is the last time. I want you to get help."

"I told you…I'm fine. Don't know why you're kicking up such a fuss about a little bit of cash."

"I've been looking at the rental income. You could be living like a king." She helped out with the Winslow Properties business, and though she wasn't in that office very often, she knew enough to realize the incoming cash was substantial. And she also knew that Harold wasn't pouring any of that money back into upkeep and development.

"You worried about your inheritance? Is that it?"

The insult barely registered. She had figured out a long time ago that her father would be lucky not to end up a pauper. "I'm worried about *you*," she said quietly. "And though you may not believe me, I'm done. No more handouts."

He backed toward the door, his posture hunted. "I may sell the Courtyard," he said defiantly. "I've had inquiries from a company called Samson Oil."

The Courtyard was an old renovated ranch several miles west of town. It included a large barn and a collection of buildings that housed a growing and thriving arts community, consisting of both studios and retail shops. The land on which the Courtyard sat increased in value day by day.

"You know selling would be a big mistake." He was threatening her. Manipulating her. Classic addict behavior.

Harold shrugged. "That's your opinion. I gotta go. See you later."

Before she could react, he disappeared. Moments later she heard the front door slam.

She sank into a kitchen chair and buried her face in her

hands. If she had stayed at Case's house, she could have avoided her father tonight.

Scarcely five minutes had passed when her doorbell rang again. *Damn it.* If Harold had come back, she was going to have a little hissy fit. She wiped her eyes with the back of her hand and stood up, grabbing a paper napkin to use as a makeshift tissue.

Rarely did she let her father get to her. But as she blew her nose, she conceded inwardly that his barbs had hit the mark. He was often a mean drunk, and tonight was no exception.

It was a distinct relief to find Amanda Battle on the other side of the door. "Come in," Mellie said.

"I won't stay long. I know it's late." Amanda slipped past her, shivering dramatically. "What happened to the warm days?" The sheriff's wife was tall and slim and full of energy.

"We're headed toward the holidays. It was bound to happen. What's up, Amanda? I doubt you came to see me for a discussion about the weather."

Amanda chuckled. "The guys are playing poker at our house. I had to get out of there for a few minutes. Besides, I need a firsthand report. Nathan called Case a little while ago to see how he's doing, but you know how men are. Case said he was fine."

"You don't believe him?"

"Parker told us Case was in bad shape. He said if you hadn't shown up at the ranch to clean yesterday and found Case, he might have ended up in the hospital."

"Well, I don't know about that. I'm glad I happened to be there. I did take dinner to him this evening. He was grumpy but overall seemed somewhat better." Better enough to flirt, anyway. Not that she was about to tell Amanda that.

"You're definitely a Good Samaritan. But don't worry. Several of his friends and their wives and girlfriends have put together a meal schedule. We won't let him starve. You're off the hook with a clear conscience. And Parker is going to keep tabs on Case's flu symptoms."

"That's great."

Mellie knew Amanda didn't mean to sound dismissive… or as if she were kicking Mellie to the curb. Even so, the unintentional message was clear. Mellie was not part of that tight-knit circle of friends. It was ridiculous to let her feelings be bruised. Maybe because she had recently gone several rounds with her father, she was feeling fragile.

Amanda glanced at her watch and sighed. "I'd better get back. I promised Nathan I'd throw together some nachos."

Mellie raised an eyebrow. "At this hour?"

"When this crew convenes, they like to pretend they're all eighteen again."

"You wouldn't have it any other way. I hear it in your voice."

Amanda shrugged, her expression sheepish. "Yeah. You know me—I love to cook for people. And these guys work so hard it's fun to see them unwind."

"Nathan is lucky to have you."

Amanda's grin was smug. "Yes, he is."

Mellie walked her friend outside, feeling unmistakably envious of Amanda's good fortune. What would it be like to be loved in such a way that you knew the other person would never let you down or disappoint you, at least not in any significant way?

Ila Winslow had been that person for Mellie. But once she was gone, Mellie had been forced to face a few cold, hard truths. Love, true love, whether familial or romantic, was rare and wonderful.

* * *

The next day dawned bright and sunny, which seemed a shame given Mellie's mood. She would have much preferred gray and gloomy so she could blame her low spirits on something other than the fact she was not going to see Case Baxter today.

She attended church and brunch with a friend, then popped by the gym for her regular yoga class. In the locker room afterward as she showered, washed her hair and changed, she felt much better. Case was a blip on her radar. No need to get all hot and bothered about a guy who wasn't even her type.

Yeah, right. Her sarcastic inner woman-child sassed her.

As was her custom, Mellie had left her cell phone in the car. No one ever needed her on Sunday, and she always relaxed more knowing that she was unplugged from the electronic world, even if only for an hour and a half.

It was a shock to return to her vehicle in the parking lot and find that her cell phone had exploded with texts.

My cleaning lady has gone missing.

Twenty minutes after that: I pay double time on Sundays. Are you interested?

Mellie stared at the screen. Interested in what? The shiver that snaked down her spine had less to do with cold air hitting her damp hair than it did the prospect of deliberately placing herself beneath Case's roof during nonbusiness hours.

Then a third text: You've already been exposed. Why not keep me company?

Why not, indeed? She slid into the driver's seat, uncertain how to answer. She decided to go with bland and professional and see what happened. I don't work on Sundays,

she texted. Hope you're feeling better. I thought I would stay out of your way for now. Once you're well, I can pick up where I left off.

She made it a habit not to text and drive, so on the way home she ignored the series of dings indicating she had new messages. It wasn't until she pulled into her garage that she let herself read Case's responses...one right after another.

I don't give a damn right now if my house is clean and organized.

I'm bored.

Give a guy a break.

How humiliating was it that her hands shook as she used her phone? Case was telling the truth. He was bored, and he thought Mellie was available. She should ignore him... pretend her cell was turned off...or invent a very important function she simply couldn't miss.

Gnawing her lip, she walked a fine line between cordial and suggestive. You sound grumpy.

Of course I'm grumpy, he shot back. I'm in solitary confinement.

You probably deserve it. Oops. That definitely sounded flirtatious. JK, she added rapidly.

Her phone stayed silent for a full two minutes. She'd offended him. Yikes.

Finally, he wrote back.

Please come see me, Mellie. I'll be on my best behavior. And you don't need to cook for me. I've got enough food here to feed an army regiment.

Well, shoot. She was a strong person, but not strong enough to say no to something she really wanted. She tapped the screen.

Okay...give me an hour. Do you need me to bring anything?

Just you.

As a woman, she was generally low maintenance. An hour should have been enough time to get ready and drive out to the ranch. But she dithered over what to wear. Finally, she chose a charcoal-gray wool skirt with knee-high black leather boots and a scoop-necked black sweater with a gray chevron pattern across the chest. Silver hoop earrings and a silver necklace with a key charm completed her look.

The outfit was probably too dressy. But she could always let him think she had worn this to church. Her mother's voice echoed in her head. *Never pretend to be something you're not, Mellie. Tell the truth, even if it hurts.*

Mellie stared in the mirror, tucking a stray fiery strand behind her ear. For a moment, she contemplated leaving her long hair loose. But that might send the wrong message. Since she wasn't exactly sure what it was that she wanted to communicate to Case Baxter, it was probably smarter not to be quite so...flamboyant.

Her hair was hard to miss. Which was why she often kept it confined to a knot on top of her head or in a ponytail. Neither style seemed appropriate for tonight. She pulled the thick mass of red and gold to the side of her neck, secured it with a hairband and let it fall over one shoulder.

As she examined her reflection in the mirror, she saw

much more than a young woman dressed up for an evening that was definitely not a date. She saw uncertainty. Maybe a slice of anxiety. Most visible, however, was the undercurrent of excitement.

Grimacing, she turned and fled before she could change her mind again about what to wear. She grabbed her coat from the closet by the front door, slid her arms into it, freed her hair and scooped up her car keys.

The early evening had turned foggy. Case's house appeared out of the gathering gloom like a regal old lady, sure of her place in the community. Lonely, perhaps, but unapologetic. A light beside the front door offered a welcoming glow.

Mellie felt her pulse wobble as she climbed the steps to the porch.

Case met her at the top of the stairs, the door half-open behind him. "It's about time," he said. When he grinned, she knew he was teasing.

"You shouldn't be outside," she said. "It's freezing."

He put an arm around her shoulders and steered her into the house. "I had to get some fresh air. It's like a tomb in here."

As he took her coat, she smiled wryly. "Nicest tomb I've ever seen."

He shrugged. "I'm still running a fever. You can't trust anything I say."

And wasn't that the crux of the matter?

She laughed because he wanted her to. Still, the irony was not lost on her. "Do you really have a temperature?"

Case stopped short and bent his head. Taking her hand, he placed it on his forehead. "See."

He wasn't kidding. "How long since you've had medicine?"

"I don't know. Four hours? Five? It's probably time."

"Case…"

"Don't scold me," he said. "It makes me hot, and I'm too weak to ravish you." He urged her along the hallway and into the den. A roaring fire in the fireplace added warmth and color to a room that was sophisticated but comfy. A silver tray laden with an assortment of decadent treats was set up on the coffee table in front of the sofa.

After surveying the chocolate-dipped strawberries, champagne and candied fruits, she shot Case an incredulous glance. "Where on earth did this come from? Your friends have outdone themselves."

He sat down rather suddenly, his face an alarming shade of white. "My friends brought fried chicken and green beans. I ordered this stuff online from a specialty shop in town."

"Ah." The small luxuries seemed an odd choice for a man recovering from the flu. But then again, her personal experience with wealthy men was practically nonexistent. Perhaps for Case, this was the equivalent of buttered popcorn and jujubes at the movie theater.

"Sit down," he said gruffly, his eyes closed. "I'll be okay in a minute."

"Did you actually eat any of the fried chicken?" she asked.

"Not yet. I took a shower."

The unspoken inference was that getting his hand-delivered meal onto a plate was more than he could handle. Poor man. "Rest for a few minutes and I'll bring your meal in here."

"Thanks."

He was trying so hard to act tough, but the flu was no respecter of persons. Even a broad-shouldered, macho, athletic guy like Case Baxter could fight back only so far before admitting defeat.

In the kitchen she saw that Case had piled a few dirty dishes in the sink. On the granite-topped island she found a large disposable aluminum pan filled with an enormous amount of fried chicken. And it wasn't from the chain restaurant in town. This was the real deal.

Her mouth watered. So much for the yoga class. Ignoring her better judgment, she fixed two plates with crisp chicken breasts, home-canned green beans and fluffy yeast rolls with butter. Who knew what her host wanted to drink? But the truth was, he should have plenty of water.

Balancing two bottles she plucked from the fridge, she picked up the plates and carried them back to the den. Her host had fallen asleep again.

She stood there looking at him for long minutes, wishing she could put a name to the yearning that tightened her throat and forced her to blink moisture from her lashes. For years she had kept an eye out, always wondering if there was some special guy out there for her. But Prince Charming never showed up.

Now…here…in the most unlikely of places, she found herself tumbling headlong into an infatuation that was sure to break her heart.

Ten

Case came awake with a start, jerking upright and wondering if he had dreamed Mellie. No...there she was. Sitting across from him. Looking young and sexy and prim, her knees pressed together and her hands folded in her lap.

"Sorry," he grimaced. "I keep doing that."

Mellie lifted a shoulder. "That's the drill. Lots of rest and plenty of fluids."

He ran a hand through his hair, wincing when the restrained motion made his head throb. "How long have I been out?"

"Only forty-five minutes."

Damn it. "And you've probably been sitting here starving."

"If I was that hungry, I wouldn't have waited for you. Give me a minute and I'll put everything in the microwave to warm it up."

"No." Once Mellie left the room, he'd probably crash again. "I'm not that picky. Let's do this."

"If you're sure…"

It occurred to him that sitting up long enough to eat was a daunting proposition, even though he was ravenous. Still, he washed the Tylenol down with the bottle of water and then started in on his chicken.

Mellie ate quietly. She was a restful woman. At least when she wasn't arguing with him. He managed half of the chicken breast, the roll and a few of the green beans before he admitted defeat. Pushing his plate away, he leaned back in the embrace of the sofa and rested his head, telling himself he was on the mend. Mind over matter. That was his mantra.

His companion looked askance at him. "You need the protein," she said.

"I had a mother. I don't need another one."

Mellie blinked, set down her fork and stood. "I'll come back when you're in a better mood."

The careful rebuke hit its mark.

"I'm sorry," he muttered. "Don't go."

She crossed her arms at her waist. "I'm getting mixed signals, Case."

"I know." It was true. He wanted to be alone to wallow in his misery, but at the same time, he was intrigued by Mellie Winslow and charmed by her matter-of-fact caring.

Her hair glowed tonight, the long strands catching light from the fixture overhead. The sweater she wore was fitted but not tight. Even so, he was well aware of her ample breasts.

"Sit down. Please. I have a proposition for you."

The expression on her face told him she was evaluating all meanings of that statement. "Um…"

"Oh, hell, Mellie. I can't even finish dinner. Do you really think I'm going to lure you into my bed?"

"Of course not," she muttered, looking anywhere but

at his face. She sat down hard on the sofa, not so much an act of will as a necessary evil, as if her legs had given out. He knew the feeling.

It was a sure bet she didn't trust him. But he had a plan to win her over. "I'd like to become a silent partner in the Keep N Clean. With my investment, you wouldn't have to wait to expand."

Mellie opened and closed her mouth like a fish gasping for oxygen. She shook her head. "No, thank you."

He stared at her, his pulse far too rapid. "Maybe you didn't understand. I'd like to give you fifty thousand dollars. It's the least I can do to repay you for playing nurse."

Now his dinner guest looked murderous. "The milk of human kindness is not for sale, Mr. Baxter. Some things in life are free."

"Has anyone ever told you that you're incredibly over-sensitive?" Aggravation made his head ache like the devil.

She stared him down, her green eyes chilled to the shade of moss. "You hired me to clean and organize your house. An ordinary business arrangement. I neither want nor need your investment money."

Though it took every ounce of energy he could muster, he levered his body off the sofa and joined her on the love seat. Her spine was so straight it was a wonder it didn't crack under the weight of her disapproval.

He rested his arm behind her shoulders. "Don't make a hasty decision, Mellie. This is what I do. I find it very rewarding to help local businesses grow."

"You don't get it."

They were so close he could see the faint, almost imperceptible veins beneath her fair skin. At her temple... in the dip above her collarbone. "So explain it to me," he urged. "I'm listening." He was trying to listen, though all he really wanted to do was kiss her.

Mellie's head was bent, her profile as simple and sweet as a Madonna's. The feelings she invoked in him, however, were a far cry from religious. More like the temptations of the damned.

She inhaled and exhaled, sliding him a sideways glance that begged for understanding. "The Keep N Clean is *mine*. I've sweated and worried and planned and strategized... every mile of the way. I could have stepped into the family business and worked alongside my father, but I needed something that belonged to me...something he couldn't ruin."

"That's pretty harsh."

"You don't know him." Her smile was bleak. "He's an alcoholic...with not the slightest interest in recovery. People in town make jokes about him. The sheriff has a cell with Harold's name on it. I didn't want to be a part of that, but..."

She ground to a halt, biting her lip, her distress almost palpable.

"But what?" He smoothed a strand of hair away from her cheek, tucking it behind her ear. Her skin was softer than a Texas sunrise, all pink and pretty and sweet.

"I can't bear to see him go completely down the abyss. So I keep giving him money. Which is stupid, because his business pulls in twice what mine does."

Her voice broke as a single tear rolled down her cheek. Mellie seemed oblivious. Case felt something twist inside his chest. He couldn't tell if it was a good feeling or a bad one...maybe just damned scary.

Pulling her head to his shoulder, he stroked her hair, releasing the band that held it and using his fingers to winnow through the fragrant mass. "Sometimes doing the right thing is really hard."

"How would you know?" The question was tart.

He rested his chin on top of her head. "My college

roommate had a drug problem, but he hid it from me for almost a year. I was constantly bailing him out of jail and making excuses for him. Until the night I came home from a date with my current girlfriend and found Toby on the floor of our apartment. Dead. From an overdose."

He recited the tale simply, even though the recounting jabbed at a spot in his heart that had never quite healed.

Mellie pulled back to look at him, her eyes wide and distraught. "Oh, Case. I'm so sorry." She put her hands on his cheeks. "You must have been devastated."

Her simple empathy reached down inside the hard shell he'd worn since his divorce and found purchase in a tiny crack. Emotions roiled in his chest, feelings he hated. It was much simpler when he saw Mellie Winslow as simply a potential bed partner. He didn't want to know her innermost secrets. He didn't want to care.

But he was lost…defeated. Almost before the battle had begun. "I want to kiss you," he said raggedly, "but I can't. I'm sick."

Her smile was both wicked and reassuring. "Then I'll kiss *you*," she whispered.

Never in his life had he let a woman take the initiative. Though he didn't mind an aggressive woman in bed if the mood was right, he liked to lead the dance. Even so, it was damned arousing to submit, even momentarily, to Mellie's slightly awkward affections.

She started with his stubbly jaw, her tongue damp against his hot skin. The feminine purr of pleasure sent every drop of blood to his sex, leaving him hard and breathless.

"Mellie?"

She ignored him. Leaning into his embrace, she nuzzled his ear, kissed his brow, traced his nose with a fingertip. When her mouth hovered over his, he protested. "No." It

might have been more convincing if he hadn't been dragging her against his chest. "I don't need your pity."

"But you want to kiss me."

It was a statement, not a question. He shuddered, his arousal viciously demanding, relentlessly insistent. *Take, take, take.* "Of course I want to kiss you," he said, the words sandpaper in his throat. Any living, breathing heterosexual male would want to kiss her.

Carefully, telling himself he was still in control, he slid a hand beneath the edge of her sweater and found the plane of her belly with his fingertips. Mellie's sharp intake of breath spurred him on. When she didn't move, not even a millimeter, he found her breast and palmed it.

Hell. Her curves were all woman. Beneath a layer of silky stuff and lace, he felt her heat, her life force. Wanting turned him inside out.

Moving slowly so as to not alarm her, he eased them into a reclining position, Mellie on her back, Case on his side—against the couch—his upper body sheltering hers.

She stared up at him, wide-eyed. "We can't do this."

He unfastened the button on the side of her skirt… lowered the zipper…exposed her practical cotton undies. "I know."

"Wait." She put a hand on his wrist. "Weren't you supposed to woo me with champagne and strawberries?"

He was shaking. Either his fever was back or he was out of control. "Dessert," he said, the words barely audible. "In a little while."

His hand moved of its own accord, breaching the inconsequential narrow barrier of elastic on her bikini underpants and sliding lower.

Mellie whimpered. There was no other word for it. In that raw, needy sound, he heard every last one of his scru-

ples and reservations spelled out. This was insane. *He* was insane.

He swallowed hard. "Shall I stop?" She would never know what the question cost him.

She held his hand against her body, gripping his wrist until her fingernails dug into his skin. The spark of pain drove his lust a notch higher. "Don't you dare."

When he found the moist cleft of her sex, they both groaned. As he stroked her gently, he felt her lift against his hand.

He was dizzy…hungover…and he hadn't even popped the cork on the bubbly. "Close your eyes, Mellie."

Mellie panted, her chest rising and falling rapidly. Why hadn't he removed her sweater? Hell, he couldn't stop now. It wouldn't be fair.

"I want to see you naked," he said urgently.

"Please, don't stop…" The three words were raspy, but ended on a sharp cry.

Watching and feeling Mellie find satisfaction was humbling. No pretenses. No big show. Just a woman experiencing pleasure—deep, raw gratification.

When she could breathe again, he rested his forehead on hers. "I want you."

She licked her lips, her expression befuddled. "You've been desperately ill. Maybe your heart's not healthy enough for sex." She dared to tease him.

"My heart's fine," he groused, not amused by her joking allusion to a television commercial. "And I don't appreciate the reference. I have the flu, not ED."

She curled her arms around his neck, smiling drowsily. "You're gorgeous even when you're sick. It's not fair. And PS, I've never done it with a cowboy."

"You *still* haven't done it," he pointed out, his disgruntlement tempered only by the fact that he felt like hell.

"They say anticipation is half the pleasure."

"I'd like a chance to find out."

"The first day you're well, I swear. We'll drink that champagne and go for it."

"Cheap advice from a woman who just—"

She clapped her hand over his mouth. "Don't be grouchy. Your time will come. In fact, if you think you're up to it, I'm right here. Carpe diem and all that."

He thought about it. Seriously. For about ten seconds. But a quick assessment of his head-to-toe misery settled the argument. "No," he sighed. "I want to impress you with my carnal prowess."

"Is that really a thing?"

"You'll have to wait and see, now, won't you?"

She frowned, examining his face, no doubt spotting the damp forehead and the sudden lack of color. "You need to be in bed," she said firmly. "Alone."

He wanted to argue. He *really* wanted to argue. But damn it, Mellie was right. "I don't want you to leave," he said. "You keep me occupied."

"That's one word for it." She sat up, forcing him to, as well. When they were hip to hip, she took his hand. "I think it's best if I put cleaning your house on hold…give you a week to recover without anyone underfoot. If you're better by the end of the week, we'll talk about resuming our original schedule."

"I *have* to be better by the weekend," he said.

"Why?"

"The club is throwing a big party Saturday night to honor me as the new president."

"Ah."

"That's all you have to say…*ah*?"

She cocked her head. "What do you want me to say?"

"You could at least act interested."

"I don't follow."

"Oh, for God's sake, Mellie. You know I want you to go with me."

She stood abruptly. "I most certainly do not. We're barely acquaintances."

"Aren't you forgetting what just happened? When I rocked your world?" He smiled to let her know he was kidding about the world-rocking thing.

Mellie actually winced. "Aside from your Texas-sized ego, what you and I have been dancing around is the possibility of a fling, *not* any kind of official status. That's crazy."

"Why won't you go with me? It's a single social occasion, not a relationship."

Her reluctance dinged his pride. It wasn't boasting to say that any one of a large number of women in Royal would be pleased to attend the upcoming party as his guest. Mellie looked as if he had offered to take her to a funeral.

"I like my life just fine, Case. Other than the occasional run-in with my dad, I'm pretty happy with the way things have turned out for me. I own a business I love… I have a lot of interesting friends. I'm not interested in finding a man to take care of me."

His temper started a slow boil. "We're talking about a *party*, Ms. Winslow. It's hardly a basis for what you're thinking about."

"True. But if we end up in bed together, I'd rather no one else know about it. That way when we're done, there won't be any messy explanations to deal with."

When we're done… Maybe if he hadn't felt so rotten, he might have been able to understand why her blithe prediction about their future bothered him so much.

"Fine," he said, his jaw clenched. "I won't ask again. If you want me, you'll have to say so. I'm done here."

Eleven

If you want me, you'll have to say so. Mellie replayed those words in her head a thousand times over the next four days. Her departure from Case's house Sunday evening was not her finest hour. He had stormed out of the room, and she had left without saying goodbye.

She was ashamed of her behavior. Her only excuse was that, even sick, Case Baxter made her jittery and uncertain about things she had always seen as rock solid in her life. For one, her assumption that having an intimate relationship with a man was something she didn't have time for.

Honestly, she worked so hard and kept so busy, she rarely thought about what she was missing. She dated now and then, but with only a couple of exceptions over the years, she'd never felt an inescapable urge to have sex just for the sake of having sex.

She thought about it. Alone at night. In the privacy of her bedroom. But her fantasy lovers were compliant and undemanding…exactly the opposite of Case Baxter.

What did he want with her?

By the time she closed the office for a late lunch on Thursday afternoon, she had brought her books up to date, signed contracts with three new clients and worked herself into a mental frenzy of uncertainty. Instead of heading home, she pointed her car in the direction of the diner.

She had to talk to someone, or she'd explode. Amanda was the logical choice.

Fortunately, the sheriff's wife was in her usual spot, smiling and swapping jokes with her regular customers. Mellie had purposely waited until almost two o'clock, hoping that the noon rush would be over and Amanda would have time for a chat. Because of the subject matter, Mellie snagged the booth in the far back corner, hoping to talk quietly without being overheard.

When the other woman headed her way, Mellie waved a hand at the opposite side of the booth. "Do you have time to take a break? I need some advice."

Amanda said a word to her second in command and slid onto the bench seat with a sigh. "Success is killing me," she said. But the smug pride on her face told a different story.

"You love it," Mellie said.

"True. What's up, girlfriend? It's not like you to drop by in the middle of the day."

Mellie played with the saltshaker, feeling the tops of her ears warm. This was embarrassing. "I may have done something stupid."

Amanda leaned in, her elbows on the table, hands clasped under her chin. "Do tell. Are we talking five-hundred-dollar-shoes stupid or forgot-to-thaw-the-chicken-for-dinner stupid?"

"It's more of a personal matter."

"Oh. My. Gosh. You've had sex."

"*No.* Well, sort of. But not really. You're missing the point."

Amanda raised an eyebrow. "Do I need to give you a lesson about the birds and the bees? Was there nudity involved? Skin-to-skin contact? At your age, I'd think you'd be pretty clear about the definition."

Mellie glanced around wildly, making sure no one was in earshot. "Lower your voice, please," she hissed. "I'd rather this not end up on the evening news."

"Who is it?" Amanda demanded. "The new wrangler over at Hartley Ranch? Or, no, it's the dentist…right? He's asked you out a half dozen times and you finally said yes."

Mellie smiled, despite her turmoil. "It's not the dentist. He kept wanting to whiten my teeth…not at all romantic."

"Then who?"

"Back up," Mellie said. "I didn't have sex. Or at least not all the way. More like teenagers in the back of a car."

Amanda appeared to be struck dumb, her eyes wide with astonishment. "It's like I don't even know you," she said.

Mellie wondered suddenly if she should have kept things to herself. But she couldn't move forward without at least an amateur second opinion. She decided to come at the situation from another angle. "I've been invited to the party at the Cattleman's Club Saturday night."

"Okayyyy… So what's the stupid thing you did?"

"I said no."

"Ah. And now you want to change your mind."

"Maybe. But what if he's already asked someone else?"

"Is that likely?"

"I'm not sure. He was mad when I turned him down. Said he wasn't going to ask again. That I would have to tell him if I wanted to go." She fudged a bit. That wasn't exactly how Case had phrased it. He'd said Mellie would have to say she wanted *him*.

"I still haven't heard a name." Amanda's brow creased.

"The *who* isn't important. Because even if I decide to contact him, I don't have a dress to wear."

"That part's easy." Amanda sat back and took a sip of the iced tea she'd brought with her to the table. "Last year when Nathan and I were invited to the governor's mansion for a law enforcement ball, I bought a dress I never wore. I decided the color didn't work for me and the skirt was way too long and too hard to hem. But the dress was on clearance, so I couldn't return it. You and I are about the same size. Plus, you're taller, so I think it will work. Why don't I bring it by your house this evening?"

"That would be great." Except that Mellie had been counting on a lack of wardrobe choices as her reason not to go to the party.

Amanda glanced at her watch. "I've gotta get back to work. I'll text you when I'm on my way...okay?"

"Sure."

Amanda stood and tapped the table with her finger. "You can't keep his name a secret forever. If the dress works, the price for my fashion donation is full disclosure."

"I don't know why you're making such a big deal about this. If I end up going, you'll find out who it is. You and Nathan will be at the party...right?"

"Of course...but I hate surprises. So you might as well tell me tonight."

By 6:00 p.m. Mellie chickened out and sent a text to Amanda.

Changed my mind about the party. Thanks anyway.

Amanda was not so easily dissuaded. She showed up at Mellie's house half an hour later, garment bag in hand.

When Mellie answered the door, Amanda frowned at her. "I never figured you for a coward."

Mellie stepped back, shrugging helplessly. "I'm not a coward. But it's complicated."

"Isn't it always?" Amanda placed the long black bag on Mellie's coffee table and sat down on the sofa.

Mellie took the chair opposite. "I've waited too long to say yes. It's a moot point now. Sorry you came for nothing."

Amanda stared at her. "Tell me who it is."

"Case." Even saying his name out loud made Mellie shiver with a combination of anticipation and dread.

"Case who? Your boss?"

Apparently, Mellie was right. The idea that Case Baxter might invite his housekeeper to the most important event of the year was inconceivable. "Yes."

At last Amanda grasped the enormity of the situation. Her jaw dropped. "Case Baxter invited you to be his date for the party honoring him as the new president of the Texas Cattleman's Club and you turned him down?" That last part ended on a screech.

Mellie winced. "Yes."

Silence reigned for long minutes. Amanda looked at Mellie as if she were some kind of alien being. "I didn't think you even knew Case until you started cleaning his house."

"I didn't. But when he got sick and I helped him out a bit, we…um…"

"Fell madly in lust with each other?"

Mellie couldn't decide if Amanda was scandalized or delighted. "I didn't even like him at first," Mellie said. "He's arrogant and bossy and opinionated…"

"In other words, a Texas male. It's in their DNA, Mellie."

"Maybe."

"But you got past that first impression, obviously."

"I still think he's all of those things, but when he was so sick, I saw another side of him. A human side. A vulnerable side."

"Oh, dear."

"What?"

"You're falling for the guy."

"Don't be silly. He's handsome, and when you get to know him, not so bad, but this isn't about anything long-term."

"So why did you turn him down?"

A very good question. "He's the guest of honor Saturday night. He'll be in the spotlight. I'm not a center-of-attention kind of girl."

"So?"

"I shouldn't even have mentioned this to you. I'm not going, so it doesn't matter."

"Try on the dress. And don't argue." Amanda could be like a dog with a bone when she wanted something.

"Fine. But only because you won't leave me alone until I do." Mellie snatched up the dress in its protective covering and hurried down the hall to her bedroom, trying to ignore Amanda's mischievous smile.

When she unzipped the garment bag, she sucked in a breath. The gown was amazing. It was halter necked and backless. The chiffon-and-silk fabric almost glowed. The color started out as sea-foam green at the bodice, edged into a slightly darker hue at the hips and continued the length of the dress, sliding from one shade into the next as the mermaid-style skirt fell in a dozen layers of tiny ruffles.

No woman could resist trying it on. With a few contortions, Mellie managed the zipper on her own and slid her

feet into strappy high heels. One look in the mirror told her the gown was made for her.

Amanda called out from the living room. "I want to see it. Come model for me."

"Give me a minute." Mellie stared in the mirror, trying to imagine the expression in Case's eyes if he saw her in this dress. She didn't suffer from false modesty. Her body was nice...average. But in this confection of multishaded green, she felt like a princess.

Amanda actually stood up and clapped when Mellie walked into the living room. "You look amazing. And I was right. The length is perfect."

"I can't wear a bra." Her shoulders and back were bare.

"You don't need one. I'm so excited you're going to the party."

Mellie held up a hand. "I haven't even tried to contact Case, and if I do, he's probably asked someone else already."

Amanda chuckled. "Why don't we find out?"

"Now?"

"Of course now. The event is less than forty-eight hours away."

"I'll text him later tonight. Let me change out of this and we can grab some dinner. Didn't you say Nathan was working tonight?"

"Yes. But I think my stomach can wait five minutes for a meal. Quit stalling."

"Be honest, Amanda. Don't you see that this could be a disaster? Gossip spreads faster than wildfire around here."

Amanda hugged her, careful not to muss the dress. "It's a very simple question. If he enjoys your company and you like being with him, all that matters is whether or not you can keep from getting hurt."

"It won't last long. He's not interested in anything serious."

"That's all the more reason to enjoy it now. You work hard, Mellie. And you deserve an exciting evening with one of Royal's premier eligible ranchers."

"Sounds like a B-grade reality show."

"I'm serious. Do the Cinderella thing for one night. And come Monday, everything can go back to normal."

"You make it sound so easy."

Amanda picked up Mellie's cell phone. "Here." She held it out. "Do it before you get cold feet."

"I already have cold feet," Mellie complained. But she took the phone and pulled up Case's contact info. Hastily, without overthinking it, she clicked out a message.

If the invitation is still open, I would like 2 go with you to the party Saturday nt.

Suddenly, she felt like throwing up. It was going to be so embarrassing when he told her it was too late…that he had invited someone else. Every passing second made her want to climb into a hole and hide.

Even Amanda seemed abashed, her romantic soul shriveling in the loud silence.

Suddenly, Mellie's phone dinged.

I'll pick you up at 6:30. Glad you changed your mind.

Heart pounding, Mellie replied.

Only about the party. Just so we're clear.

Chicken?

No. Practical. How R U feeling?

100%. Good enough to rock your world. ☺

"What's going on over there?" Amanda asked when Mellie giggled.

Who knew a man like Case Baxter would use an emoticon?

Mellie sat down on the sofa, her legs suddenly too weak to hold her up. "Um, nothing special. He says he's glad I changed my mind."

"Well, there you go. You were worried for nothing."

Maybe. Or maybe her worries were only beginning.

Twelve

Friday flew by in a blur. Mellie subbed for one of her ladies, worked on her scheduling for three weeks out and at the end of the day went for a mani-pedi at her favorite salon.

That night she fell into bed, too exhausted to worry about her upcoming date with Case. But Saturday morning, the day of reckoning arrived. She and Amanda met after lunch to get their hair done.

They had booked simultaneous appointments. Amanda requested that her hair be arranged in a soft knot on top of her head with tendrils framing her face. She would look adorable.

The salon owner and Amanda ganged up on Mellie when Mellie asked for a similar style. "Yours needs to be down and wavy," Amanda insisted. "That gorgeous color will pop against the green of the gown."

"And who says I want to *pop*?"

The other women ignored her, their plan already in progress.

An hour later it was done.

Mellie had asked for a trim, but her hair still swung softly against her shoulders. She paid for her session and waited as Amanda did the same. The truth was, she *did* feel a little bit glamorous.

They saw several other women in the shop, as well—ranchers' wives mostly, with a few girlfriends thrown in. Tonight these would be the people observing Case and his date.

On the sidewalk, Mellie parted company with Amanda. "Promise you'll rescue me at the party if things get weird."

Amanda laughed, her cheeks pink from the heat inside. "Nothing is going to get weird, but yes… Nathan and I will look out for you."

After that somewhat reassuring promise, Mellie went home and second-guessed her decision a thousand times. When she was stressed, she liked to clean, so that's what she did. After a couple of hours, her house was spotless. But she was still jittery.

When Case arrived to pick her up, Mellie felt as awkward as a preteen on her first date. She opened the door and managed not to swoon. He stood there filling the entryway…tall, incredibly handsome, king of his domain in the conservative tux that fit his long, lean body to perfection. Clearly, he was on the mend.

His lazy grin lit a spark deep inside her. She wanted to gobble him up but at the same time had the urge to run away.

He must have nicked himself shaving. She could see the tiny red spot where he had managed to staunch the trickle of blood.

As she stepped back so that he could come in, his warm

gaze raked her from head to toe. "Hello, Mellie." His tone was low and intimate. "You look stunning." The words held a level of intensity she hadn't anticipated.

"Thank you," she muttered. "I'm ready. All I need to do is grab my wrap."

Case was fully recovered from the flu, but he still felt a little unsteady on his feet. Mostly from lying around all week. Inactivity wasn't his usual style.

The fact that Mellie had changed her mind about being his date tonight gave him great hope for the culmination of the evening. Now that he was well, he wasn't about to let her get away a second time. All he'd been able to think about as the days dragged by this week was how amazing it had been to hold Mellie and kiss her and how desperately he wanted to do so much more.

If it had been up to him, the club wouldn't be throwing a party in his honor this evening. But he understood that his new title came with certain social obligations. Having Mellie at his side would go a long way toward making the evening's festivities palatable. Despite her reservations about being seen in public with him, he was going to be proud to have her on his arm tonight.

Thank God he was finally well. Everything was going according to plan.

As she disappeared down the hallway, he watched her go, taking note of the way her dress dipped low in the back. His breath came faster and his forehead was damp, but his symptoms had nothing at all to do with the flu. Mellie Winslow was a smart, gorgeous, funny woman.

And for tonight she was his.

By the time he had tucked her into his vintage sports car, he realized two things. One, he should have brought the larger Mercedes. He and Mellie were so close in this

small space he could have leaned over and kissed her with no trouble at all. Given the fact that he was already hard just from looking at her and inhaling her light scent, he was in trouble.

Secondly, Mellie was as nervous as a long-tailed cat in a room full of rocking chairs. She seemed pale, but maybe that was a trick of the light. "Relax," he said. "We're going to a party. I want you to have fun."

Mellie half turned in her seat. "I don't know why I let you talk me into this." Her eyes were huge. The pulse at the base of her throat beat rapidly.

He smiled, ruefully aware that he was in far deeper than he wanted to admit. What he was about to do would make them late, but it would be worth it. Leaning across the gearshift, he held her chin in one hand and slid his other hand beneath her masses of golden-red hair to cup her nape. "I can't wait all night to taste you."

He kissed her slowly, even though he wanted to do the opposite. Her lip gloss would have to be repaired, but that was a minor inconvenience. She responded instantly, moving toward him and sighing as his tongue mated with hers. Her skin was soft and warm, her kiss feminine and eager.

Damn. His memories hadn't been exaggerated by his illness at all. Here he was, stone-cold sober, fever-free and wildly out of control already. He inhaled sharply and released her, pausing only to run his thumb along her trembling lower lip. "Say something," he demanded.

Her faux-fur wrap had fallen away. Mellie retrieved it and huddled into the warmth. "Like what?"

Now that her bare shoulders were covered, maybe he could manage a coherent conversation. "I want to strip that dress from your body and drag you into the backseat."

So much for conversation.

Mellie managed a smile. "I'd invite you inside, but I

think it's probably a terrible faux pas for the newly elected president of the Texas Cattleman's Club to miss his own party."

He gripped the steering wheel, needing to refute her statement but knowing she was right. "Afterward. Tonight. I want to stay over."

The silence lasted several beats too long for his peace of mind. Mellie wrinkled her nose. "I'd rather you not. My neighbors are nosy."

Hell. "Be honest with me, Mellie. Are you objecting to the venue or to the idea of you and me?"

This time her answer was even slower in coming. "The venue only, I suppose. I'd like to think I could say no to you, but I won't lie to myself. I want you, Case. But we seem to be at an impasse, because I know you don't have women spend the night out at the ranch."

A knot inside his chest relaxed. "For you, I'll make an exception." He meant his response to be light and teasing, but the six words came out sounding like a vow.

Mellie nodded slowly. "Okay, then. We can swing by here later, and I'll pack a bag. If you're sure."

He wasn't sure at all…about anything…except that before midnight, Mellie Winslow was going to be in his bed.

Mellie felt as if she had fallen down the rabbit hole. Suddenly, her career seemed far less important than her love life. Since when did she calmly make plans to spend the night with a man? She hadn't had sex in over two years. Maybe she should warn Case that she was rusty. Or maybe he knew enough for the both of them.

As they pulled up in front of the imposing Texas Cattleman's Club, a uniformed parking valet hurried forward, ready to take the keys and whisk the car away. Case helped

Mellie out of the low-slung vehicle, both of them taking care not catch her dress on anything.

When she stood at his side, her stomach full of butterflies, he slipped an arm around her waist. "You ready?"

She nodded, but her heart plummeted. Out at the ranch, Case had simply been a sick male who needed her help. Now…here…it was going to be impossible to ignore who he really was.

That truth was hammered home with a vengeance as they stepped through the doors of the club. Camera flashes went off in chorus. Reporters shouted questions. Case gave the press crew an easy smile and a good sound bite, even as he kept his arm curled protectively around Mellie and steered them toward the ballroom, stopping only to drop off Mellie's wrap and clutch purse at the coat-check counter.

Another doorway, another entrance.

This time there were no cameras, but instead a surge of well-wishers who wanted to congratulate Case. It was inevitable that he and Mellie would end up separated. She smiled and wiggled her fingers at him to let him know she was okay. It was actually kind of sweet to see how many people gathered around him to say hello.

As she waited for the crush to subside, Mellie looked around the room with curiosity. This was only the third time in her life she'd ever been inside the club, and the other two occasions had been long ago.

The building was a century old and had been cared for well over the years. Tradition mingled with luxury seamlessly. It was fun to see so many people dressed to the nines and ready to party.

Mellie smoothed her skirt and kept a smile on her face. Just as she was planning to go in search of an out-of-the-

way corner, strong fingers gripped her elbow. "You're not getting rid of me that easily."

"Case." She was startled to find him at her side. A moment ago he'd been surrounded by a small crowd of people.

"I want you to meet Mac McCallum," he said. "And his sister Violet. Mac is an energy technology whiz. Violet keeps their family ranch running smoothly."

Mellie shook hands with each of the attractive McCallum siblings. "Lovely to meet you both."

Violet grinned. "I think this is going to be a short-lived conversation. They're motioning for the two of you to lead out the first dance of the evening."

Mellie's mouth went dry. She looked up at Case as they made their way to the center of the room. "Do you even know how to dance?" she whispered. "'Cause I'm not exactly a professional."

"My mother and grandmother were old school. Young men had an obligation to learn the ways of gentlemen. Dancing was at the top of the list."

"I'm impressed."

The orchestra stuck up a dreamy tune as Case swept Mellie into his arms. At some level she was aware that she and Case were alone in the middle of the floor. Overhead, a priceless chandelier sparkled, showering them with small rainbow flashes of light. The crowd was four- and five-people deep, pressed back around the edges of the room.

But in Case's arms she forgot to be either nervous or self-conscious. He held her confidently, steering her easily in a waltz. His hand was warm on her back. "Thank you for coming with me tonight," he said, his smile a flash of white in his tanned face. "You've made this a lot more fun for me."

"You didn't really need a date," she pointed out. "There

are all sorts of women in this room who would love to dance with you."

He dipped her skillfully and laughed when she couldn't stifle a small gasp. "I didn't want any of them," he said. "I only want you."

After that, the song ended and everyone took the floor as the next song began.

Case bent to whisper in her ear. "Let's get something to eat."

She nodded, even as he extricated them from the mass of bodies nearby. Fortunately, the air was cooler and the people fewer as they approached the buffet tables. Mellie filled her plate with boiled shrimp, beautiful canapés and various hors d'oeuvres. "This looks amazing."

Case served himself three times as much, but then again, he was a big man who needed a lot of fuel. He found a table for two. "Eat fast," he joked. "More of my friends want to meet you."

Mellie knew the moment alone wouldn't last long. It seemed as if every eye in the room was on them. Her earlier reservations about being seen in public with Case Baxter came flooding back. "It's easy to see why you were elected," she said. "You're very popular."

He lifted an eyebrow as he wolfed down a spicy meatball. "It would be the same for anyone who holds this position. People like knowing they have access to influence."

"That's a pretty cynical statement."

"But true. I learned a long time ago not to believe my own press. When a man has money and power, people flock around like bees to honey. Underneath it all, I'm just a Texas cowboy."

"If you say so." Maybe he was being modest and maybe he really believed what he said. Either way, he wasn't seeing clearly. There was something special about Case…

something that made her want to be with him for more than a single night. Something elemental. Something real.

She didn't particularly enjoy the barrage of eyes trained on their table at the moment. The avid interest made her worry about finding food in her teeth or spilling wine on her beautiful dress. Still, it was a relief to know that she didn't feel as out of place as she had expected.

When they finished eating, Case began to introduce her to an endless stream of his friends, including Jeff Hartley, a local rancher who appeared to be without a date for the party, and Drew and Beth Farrell, to name a few. Some of them—such as Dr. Reese—Mellie knew already, at least in passing.

Royal wasn't all that big. Families tended to own the same land for generations. Drew and Beth shared the story of how they had been not-so-friendly neighbors until the wicked F4 tornado stranded them together in a storm cellar.

All of Case's circle of friends were interesting people. Beneath the social chitchat, though, Mellie knew what Case was thinking. Because she was thinking about it, too. Sex. Naked, wild, exploratory sex. Two people attracted to each other without much else in common.

When Case was pulled into a conversation that seemed to be more business than pleasure, Mellie hung back on the far edges of the room, listening to the band and chatting with Amanda and Nathan. Unfortunately, her support team was heading out early.

Amanda hugged Mellie. "It's been a fun evening, but Nathan was up at five this morning. We're going home."

Mellie returned the hug. "Thank you again for the dress. I think Case likes it."

Nathan snorted. "Every man in the room likes it. You're a knockout, Mellie Winslow."

"Hey." Amanda pinched her husband's arm. "I'm standing right here."

He scooped her up and gave her a thorough kiss, one that left Amanda pink cheeked and starry-eyed. "Mellie knows I only have eyes for you, sweetheart. Don't you, Mellie?"

"I do. And she feels the same way about you. Now go home before you get arrested for public indecency."

Their laughter was equal parts smug and rueful.

Watching the Battles walk across the dance floor to the exit gave Mellie a funny twinge in her chest. Amanda and Nathan had known each other forever. Their relationship was rock solid, and they were more in love today than they had ever been.

What would it be like to have that kind of security and trust in a relationship?

She was still rattling that question around in her head when a young cowboy came up to her and asked for a dance. He couldn't have been more than twenty-one or twenty-two. Mellie felt ancient in comparison, but his earnest invitation was sweet.

They moved around the dance floor in silence. The young cowhand seemed nervous, because he glanced in Case's direction now and then. "Mr. Baxter is giving me the evil eye," he said.

"Don't mind him. You and I are having a nice dance. Nothing wrong with that."

"Your dad is Harold Winslow, right?"

Mellie stumbled slightly. "Um, yes. Why do you ask?" Now the invitation made more sense.

The kid cleared his throat. "My cousin owns one of the shops out at the Courtyard. Word got around this week that your dad is thinking of selling the place. It's made folks nervous about their businesses. When I saw you here to-

night, I thought I'd get an answer straight from the horse's mouth."

"You might want to rethink that comparison," Mellie said drily.

The cowhand blushed. "You know what I mean. Is it true?"

Mellie mulled over her answer. "It may be true that my father has been talking big and throwing his weight around. But I'm part owner of the company, too, and as far as I know, there are no plans to sell. Who is your cousin, anyway?"

"Raina Patterson. She owns the antiques store Priceless."

"Oh, yes... I know her. Please tell Raina I'll be out to see her in the next couple of weeks to set things straight. And tell her she has a sweet cousin."

Now the wrangler's neck and ears were as red as the stripe in his Western shirt. "Thank you, ma'am. Nice dancing with you."

Mellie had no sooner grabbed a glass of punch than Case appeared at her side again. For a big man, he surely was quiet and fast when he wanted to be. "Should I bow or salute?" she asked. "Now that you're officially the president and all?"

He snagged her glass and took a sip, his lips landing exactly where hers had been. "I saw the young pup encroaching on my territory. Don't you know you're supposed to throw the small ones back in the water?"

"Very funny. He's a sweetheart."

"I'll bet. He was one of the brave ones. Every unattached guy in this room is thinking about doing what he did."

"You do know how to flatter a girl." She smiled, her confidence buoyed by Case's wry observations.

Case lifted an eyebrow when a tall man with shaggy brown hair and green eyes approached them. The man gave Mellie an appreciative glance. "I don't know how you ended up dancing with Case," the man said, "but I'd be love to take a turn on the dance floor with you, pretty lady."

"Well, I—"

"This one's taken," Case said, glowering. He glanced at Mellie. "Meet my buddy Logan Wade. He likes fast horses and fast women, not necessarily in that order."

Mellie laughed. "Nice to meet you, Logan."

Logan shook her hand, his grip warm and firm. "Don't listen to him. I'm harmless. Case is the ladies' man in our group. At least I'm not opposed to marriage on principle."

From the look on Case's face, he wasn't amused by his friend's ribbing.

Case glanced at his watch. "I've done my time," he muttered. "Mellie and I are going to get out of here. This crowd will party for several more hours."

Logan kissed Mellie's hand theatrically. "When you get tired of this guy, give me a call."

Thirteen

Case's mood soured. Was Mellie tempted by Logan Wade's offer? Surely not. But the other man was definitely popular with women. They loved his easy-going personality.

Case shoved aside the unwelcome realization that Mellie might be looking for something more than Case wanted to offer. He had enjoyed the evening more than he'd thought he would. But right now he was focused on the after-party.

He hoped Mellie was on the same page, because he was wired and hungry. For a brief moment he thought about heading straight to the ranch. It was possible once they got to Mellie's house, she would change her mind.

At a stop sign, in the glare of a streetlight, he studied her profile. "Penny for your thoughts," he said lightly. Surely she wasn't actually thinking about Logan's smooth flirtation. The other rancher was only trying to needle Case.

When she gave Case her full attention, her luminous,

deep eyes drew him in. For a moment, he thought she wasn't going to answer. Then she drew a visible breath. "Will you tell me about your wife?"

The question was way down on the list of things he'd expected her to say. "Is that a prerequisite for tonight?"

"I didn't mean to make you angry."

"I'm not angry," he said, gripping the steering wheel. "But it's old news."

"I'd still like to know. Please…"

He shrugged, wishing he had loosened his bow tie. "I was young and stupid. Leslie worked for my dad. She saw me as a meal ticket, I guess. Dad tried to warn me… suggested a prenup. But I refused. We'd been married for six months when Leslie cleaned out two of my bank accounts and skipped the country."

"I am so sorry. You must have been devastated."

"She didn't break my heart, if that's what you're thinking. But she sure as hell damaged my pride and my self-respect."

"Because you couldn't see through her?"

"Yeah. I guess I wanted to believe I was irresistible."

"You are, as far as I'm concerned. I'm not in the habit of having *sleepovers* with men I've known all of about ten minutes."

In her voice he heard an echo of the same reservations that plagued him. He pulled up in front of her house and put the car in Park. "This isn't the norm for me, either, Mellie. And I might point out that I offered you fifty grand as an investment, but you turned it down. So I'm hoping it's my charm and wit that won you over."

As an attempt at humor, it fell flat.

Mellie's small white teeth worried her lower lip. "Maybe that was a ploy on my part to get you to trust me."

"Go get your toothbrush," he urged, his voice hoarse. "I can't wait much longer."

She stared at him, her hands plucking restlessly at the tiny ruffles on her skirt. Despite their current locale, she reminded him of a mermaid, luring a man into the deep.

"Is this a one-night stand, Case?"

"It's not anything yet." He sighed. "I can't imagine letting you go after only one night."

"But you agree that the two of us are temporary."

His temper boiled over, exacerbated by lust and uncertainty. "Damn it, Mellie. Do you want this or not?"

She swallowed, and he saw her chest rise and fall. "Wait here," she said. "I'll be back."

Twelve minutes and thirty-seven seconds. That was how long it took. When he saw the door to her house open, he jumped out of the car and met her, taking the small overnight bag and tossing it in the trunk.

She was still wearing her mermaid gown, which was a good thing, because he had fantasies of all the ways he wanted to peel the silky fabric away from her creamy-skinned body. He helped her into the car, waited until she tucked her skirt inside and closed the door.

The drive out to the ranch was silent. The miles ticked by rapidly. His brain was a jumble of wants and needs and more angst than was warranted in advance of a simple sexual encounter.

When he pulled up in front of his house, he realized he'd forgotten to leave a single light on. Through the windshield, he saw the night sky punctuated with a million stars. One of the many things he loved about living in Texas was the immensity of the universe overhead.

Every male instinct he possessed urged him to drag Mellie up the stairs and into his bed ASAP. But he wanted

to woo her, to win her trust, to make her comfortable with him.

"Can you walk in those shoes?" he asked.

She nodded. "As long as we're not talking a marathon."

"I want to show you something."

Once they were out of the car, he took her hand in his and led her toward the small corral to the left of the house. Though it was often empty, tonight a single horse stood sentinel.

"This is Misty," he said. "I bought her recently. I thought you and I might ride together sometime."

The small mare whinnied and cantered toward them, her tale swishing in the cool night air.

Mellie leaned on the fence rail, her expression animated. "She's beautiful. But I don't know how to ride."

Case raised an eyebrow. "A Texas woman who can't handle a horse? Shame on you." He lifted her by the waist and set her on the railing. Her skirt fluttered around his arms like a swarm of butterflies. "I'd love to teach you... if you're willing."

His guest's smile was demure. "I'm sure you could teach me all sorts of things."

And just like that, he reached his limit. Moving between her legs, he dragged her head down for a kiss. Hot and hard and deep. The mare lost interest and wandered away. Case lost his head and wandered into dangerous territory.

Mellie in the shimmer of the moonlight was just about the prettiest thing he'd ever seen. Her hair was more pale gold than red in this moment. And her skin glowed like pearls.

"Inside," he groaned. "Where there's a bed."

Her husky laugh inflamed him. "I thought you'd never ask."

As he lifted her down from her perch, he couldn't bear to let her go. Instead, he scooped her into his arms and carried her toward the stairs that led to the porch.

Mellie curled one arm around his neck. He smelled her, felt her, tasted her on his tongue. Everything about the night turned mystical and enchanting. And he'd never once seen himself as a whimsical man.

He caught his toe on the second step and nearly sent them both to disaster. But he managed to find his balance. "Sorry," he muttered.

She put a hand on his cheek, her fingertips cool against his hot skin. "I'm not complaining. This is my very first experience with being swept off my feet. I think you're doing just fine."

Managing the final few stairs with only a little hitch in his breathing, he set her down long enough to fish the house key out of his pocket. "*Fine* is a sucky adjective."

He pulled her into the house and flipped the lock, backing his lovely guest up against the barrier that separated them from the outside world. Taking one of her delicate wrists in each of his big hands, he raised her arms over her head and pinned her to the door. "I don't know where to start," he said, utterly serious. "I've dreamed about you every night for a week."

"I hope the reality isn't a disappointment. I haven't done this in a very long time."

His lips quirked. "I'm told it's like riding a bike."

"Or a big, strong cowboy?" The deliberately naughty challenge nearly broke him.

"It's a long night," he said. "I don't want us to peak too early."

"*Peak*? Interesting choice of words."

"Shut up and let me kiss you," he groaned. He wasn't holding her all that tightly. One wiggle or protest from

Mellie and she would be free. But to his everlasting relief, she didn't seem to mind being his captive.

He pressed the weight of his lower body against hers. Still holding her arms over her head, he kissed the side of her neck, nuzzled the spot just below her ear. "You put something in my food last week," he complained. "Some drug that makes me want you incessantly."

She nipped his chin with sharp teeth. "I'm no femme fatale. Maybe you've been on a celibate streak. Maybe I'm available. Maybe you're grateful that I didn't leave you alone to suffer that first night."

He had to let her go so he could touch her. Reverently, he covered her breasts with his hands. Clearly she wasn't wearing a bra. And just as clearly, her firm, young flesh was made for his caress. Her nipple budded beneath the silky fabric as he brushed his thumb back and forth.

"I don't know what it is," he admitted. "And I don't care. But I need you tonight, Mellie. More than you know."

Again he picked her up, and again her head came to rest over his heart. He traversed the halls of his quiet dark house by memory, avoiding furniture and other pitfalls. In his bedroom, he paused. Mellie hadn't said a word. Was she shy? Having second thoughts?

"Talk to me," he said. "Tell me what you want."

The drapes at the windows were open wide. In the ambient light he saw enough of her smile to be reassured that she wanted the same things he did, though she didn't obey his demand for her to speak.

Gently, he set her on her feet and spun her around until he could reach the single fastening at the nape of her neck. He slipped the beaded button free of the buttonhole and eased the entire bodice of the dress to her waist.

The room was hushed, every molecule of air quivering with anticipation. Opposite them, the mirror over his

dresser reflected a ghostly tableau. When he embraced her from behind and dragged her back against his pelvis, they both groaned.

It was torture to shape her bare breasts with his hands. He wanted to see her fully, but there was something wickedly sensual about their dim, shadowy figures in the glass.

At last he turned her to face him. A few inches of zipper at the base of her spine gave way beneath his questing fingers, and then he held her hand as she stepped out of the dress.

She tapped his throat with a fingertip. "Your turn."

He had to wait, chest heaving as she fumbled with his bow tie and unfastened the studs down his front. When that was done, he shrugged out of his jacket and shirt and tossed them aside far more recklessly than he had her soft gown.

With Mellie standing in front of him clad in nothing but stilettos and undies, he was a wreck. "Time out," he croaked.

At this particular moment he didn't have either the patience or the fortitude to make it through a slow undressing. He kicked off his shoes, ripped off his socks, and shucked his pants and boxers in short order.

Totally nude, he snagged her wrist and drew her back into his embrace. "Leave the shoes on," he begged.

"Whatever you want, cowboy." Her voice was warm as honey on a summer day. He heard arousal and humor in equal measures.

His erection bobbed eagerly against her belly, but she didn't seem to mind. He ran his hands over her satin-covered butt, imagining all the ways he was going to take her. "This first round might be fast and furious, but we've got all night." It was a promise and a reminder to himself. He could afford to be patient...maybe.

One last time, he indulged in the pleasure of carrying her, this time to the king-size bed. He flipped back the covers and deposited her on the mattress. After striking a match to the small candle on the bedside table, he lowered himself at her side and splayed a hand against her flat belly. "I have condoms," he said flatly. "I would never take chances with you."

He wanted her to know she could trust him.

Mellie wasn't shy. At least not anymore. One hand closed around his shaft and stroked lazily.

He sucked in a sharp breath, mortifyingly close to embarrassing himself. "Let's save that part for later, darlin', when I'm not so trigger-happy."

She released him. "If you say so."

The only reason he'd been at all able to hold himself in check was that he'd let her keep her last item of clothing. But now it was time for the panties to go. When he slid them down her legs, the nylon snagged on the sharp heel of one shoe. "I'll buy you more," he swore. "A dozen pairs in every color of the rainbow."

Without warning, she rolled to her stomach, arms cradling her head. "You could massage my back," she said, her voice muffled. "All that standing and dancing in heels isn't easy." She bent her knees and crossed her ankles in the air, taunting him with the sexy pose.

At least he thought that was what she was doing. Maybe she didn't understand how damned sexy she looked. Telling himself he was no rookie kid in the bedroom, he straddled her waist and settled his thumbs on either side of her spine. With firm pressure, he moved from her bottom to her shoulders in steady increments.

Mellie's hands fisted in the sheets. "Damn, you're good," she mumbled. "This is better than sex."

He caressed every inch of her back. Up and down. Back and forth. "Not even close."

When her body was lax and warm, he reached for the handful of small foil packets he'd put in easy reach. He sheathed himself rapidly, then flipped her to her back and positioned himself between her legs.

Mellie watched him, eyelids drooping, cheekbones flushed with color, arms over her head. "You're a very beautiful man," she said quietly, her gaze raking him from chest to groin.

Gripping her hips, he shoved deep in one forceful thrust. He didn't realize he had closed his eyes until he saw tiny yellow spots of light that pulsed in time with his heartbeat. The fit was perfect.

In retrospect, perhaps he should have started with something more original than missionary position sex. But honestly, his brain circuits were shot to hell and back. Already he needed to come. Needed it more than air and water and food. But he battled the urge.

He wanted Mellie as hungry as he was…and as desperate for the pleasure that hovered just out of reach. His hands were dark against her white skin. He liked touching her…liked the notion that she had come to his home… to his bed.

Later, perhaps, he would remember his rules. And wonder why he'd broken them for someone he'd met only a few weeks ago. But now it didn't matter.

Now she was everything he wanted and needed.

He moved in her slowly, controlling the joining of their bodies with a firm grip, loving the way her eyelids fluttered shut as her breathing quickened. "This is only the beginning," he muttered.

Mellie arched her back, her rose-tipped breasts quivering as he picked up the pace. "Promises, promises."

How could she make him smile in the midst of blind lust? He changed the angle slightly and felt the moment she caught her breath. Knowing she was with him, teetering on the brink, he let go, shuddered and collapsed into the storm.

Fourteen

Mellie couldn't breathe. The problem originated in one of two sources. Either her condition was the aftermath of a wildly lush and powerful orgasm, or it was due to the fact that a large, heavy man lay on top of her, apparently comatose.

She allowed herself a smug smile. For a woman who was out of practice in the bedroom, she hadn't done half-badly. Of course, in all honesty, most of the credit had to go to Case. Alpha males might be stubborn and aggravating and impossibly bossy, but in certain situations, it was nice to have a man with confidence. A man who could play a woman's body as if only he knew the tune.

In the quiet of the bedroom, she cataloged the situation. She needed to go pee, but she didn't want to move. She took in Case's bed…Case's bedroom…Case's big warm frame sprawled in her arms. If she were a cat, she'd be purring right now.

A river of feelings moved through her veins. Relaxation. Joy. Quiet amazement. For once, she had ignored her cautious instincts and let nature take its course. Most of the time, she ran a tight ship. Work. Home. Work and more work. Losing her mother as a teenager had left her with a need for security. And Harold was never going to be any help there.

But holding things together all the time was difficult. She'd become a grown-up before she had a chance to make teenage mistakes. Maybe she was regressing. Maybe Case Baxter was her adolescent blunder. Sleeping with a client wasn't exactly the most professional move she'd ever made…

Suddenly, her lover groaned and rolled onto his back. She held her breath until he settled back to sleep. When his breathing was even and deep again, she slipped from the bed and tiptoed naked into his bathroom, then eased the door shut behind her.

After taking care of business, she found a thick navy robe on the back of the door and slid her arms into it. She had to roll up the sleeves and belt the waist tightly, but it at least gave her some protection from the vulnerability of prancing around stark naked.

Her reflection in the mirror made her wince. Wild hair, mascara smudges, whisker burns on her neck. Her thighs tightened at the memory of Case nibbling his way from her ear to shoulder.

In hindsight, it might have been prudent to actually bring her overnight case *inside*. Fat lot of good it was doing her out in Case's car. But then again, she and Case had been too busy cavorting in the romantic moonlight to worry about pedestrian realities like toothbrushes and nighties.

When she turned out the bathroom light and prepared to

slip back into bed, her stomach growled loudly. She'd been too nervous to eat much at the party, and lunch today had been slim, as well. Fortunately, she knew her way around Case's kitchen. And she knew how much food his friends had brought over while he was sick.

As she reached into the fridge for a container of cold chicken, two big hands grabbed her butt. She yelped and spun around. "Case!"

He gave her a mock scowl. "I woke up and you were gone." Then his eyes narrowed. "Is that my robe you're wearing?"

She flushed. Case had on nothing but a pair of cotton pajama pants. His big bare feet were sexy, which meant she was in real trouble. Because she'd never been turned on by feet before. "My overnight bag is still in the car."

Case grabbed the ends of the terrycloth belt and drew her against him. "My robe never looked so good." He lowered his head and kissed her, long and sweet, making her toes curl against the cold ceramic-tile kitchen floor.

She twined her arms around his neck. Without shoes, the difference in their height was magnified. He made her feel fragile and cherished. She'd always been proud of her self-sufficiency. But it turned out there was something to be said for the notion of allowing a big, strong man to take charge once in a while.

She buried her nose in his bare shoulder. He smelled of soap and warm male skin and sex. "I was raiding your leftovers," she said.

He chuckled, the sound reverberating through her when he kissed the top of her head. "You don't really want cold chicken, do you…"

It was more a statement than a question. She raked her fingernail across his flat copper-colored nipple. "Is there a better offer on the table?"

"Maybe." He inhaled sharply. "If I feed you popcorn, will you come back to bed afterward?"

"I could be persuaded."

He picked her up by the waist and set her on top of the butcher-block island. Moments later he had the microwave humming. The scent of hot popcorn filled the air.

When it was done, Case opened a bottle of wine, poured two glasses and hopped up to sit beside her, handing her the bowl of popcorn. "It doesn't take much to make you happy, does it?"

Mellie shrugged. "We all have our weaknesses. But I like to think I'm a realist. The most important things in life are free."

He was quiet for a long time. What was he thinking?

This huge, wonderful house was a lonely cave for a man to rattle around in. He should have a wife and several children to keep him company. Then again, some guys liked being bachelors.

"May I ask you a personal question?" she asked.

Case drained his wineglass and set it aside. "Sure. Fire away."

"With your parents gone, how do you celebrate Thanksgiving?" The holiday was less than a week away.

"I don't really." Case shrugged. "I have an aunt and uncle in Austin. They always invite me, and sometimes I accept. Other years I go skiing with friends in Colorado."

"Have you celebrated any holiday in this house since your parents died?"

"No."

When he didn't elaborate, she knew she had hit a nerve. "Would you let me cook for you next week? Nothing fancy…just turkey and dressing and maybe a pie or two."

"You don't have to feel sorry for me, Mellie. I've been thinking about Thanksgiving, too. But I thought we could

head down to Key West for the long weekend. Rent a boat.
Sail around the islands. Eat fresh seafood and dance under
the stars."

"Sounds like a movie. Way too good to be true." Did he
feel the need to impress her? Or was the idea of having a
woman cook for him too domestic…too *familiar*? "Never
mind," she said lightly. "It was just a thought."

When he put a hand on her bare knee, she jumped. The
sides of her robe had gaped, allowing him a glimpse of her
legs covered in gooseflesh.

"We need to get you back in bed," he said. "Before you
catch pneumonia."

The change of subject was awkward, but she let it slide.
"Bed sounds nice." And maybe round number two. Her
snack had revived her. Leaving the door open for other
hungers to be sated.

They walked hand in hand to the bedroom. A yawn
caught her unawares.

Case laughed. "I'll let you sleep first."

"First?"

"Before round two."

Scrambling onto the mattress, she shed his robe and
held out her arms. "I can sleep when I'm dead."

This time she took the initiative. She pulled Case by
the wrist. "Lie down on your back," she said. "It's my turn
to play tour guide."

"Whatever the lady wants."

The words were playful, but the fierce light in his eyes
was anything but. His hard body quivered, poised for ac-
tion. When Mellie reclined beside him and delicately licked
the head of his shaft, he cursed and groaned. It was heady
stuff to make the mighty Case Baxter weak and needy.

She stroked him with two hands. He was a big man
everywhere.

Moments later he grabbed her wrist in an iron hold. "Enough." The glazed expression in his eyes told her what he wanted.

With only a second or two to decide if she was feeling sexually adventurous tonight, she moved over him and sat on his upper thighs. "I like having you at my mercy," she whispered. The sense of being in control was false. She knew that. Case Baxter might be a Texas gentleman, but in certain situations, the veneer of civilization wore thin.

His chest rose and fell rapidly. His cheekbones carried a flush of color, and his eyes were so dark the pupils were barely discernible. "I'll let you call the shots on this one, Mellie. Be my guest."

The words were lazy and compliant, but his hands fisted at his hips and cords of muscles flexed in his arms. The lion wasn't sleeping…merely biding his time.

After she reached for a condom, she opened it and rolled it over Case's erection. Then rising onto her knees, she lowered herself and took him deep. He'd given her one outstanding orgasm already, but she was greedy. She wanted more.

Case cursed and grabbed her ass in a bruising grip. "Don't move," he begged.

Was he really so susceptible to her charms? It seemed unlikely. Mellie possessed a healthy self-esteem, but she knew Case had access to more women than was good for him. Money, good looks, Texas cowboy charm…the trifecta wasn't really fair to the female sex.

She had to question his ex-wife's intelligence.

Mellie rested her hands, palms flat, on her lover's chest, feeling the heat of him, the light dusting of hair, the tough, muscled breadth of him. She'd told herself a hundred times that she could play this game and not get hurt. But suddenly, a knot lodged in her throat.

When had she let him become so human? When had he ceased to be the wealthy, powerful president of the Texas Cattleman's Club? When had she forgotten he could buy and sell the Keep N Clean a hundred times over and never miss the cash?

Her enjoyment of the intimate moment wavered.

Case—damn him—noticed instantly. "What's wrong?" he demanded.

"Nothing."

He grimaced. "The universal female response. And you don't sell it any better than the next woman. Talk to me, Mellie."

Unexpectedly, a wave of bittersweet regret rolled over her. Hot tears stung the backs of her eyes, but she'd have died before letting him see. "I'm fine," she whispered. "Great, in fact. Just tired."

"I'll let you sleep soon," he swore. "But first, my turn…"

Case knew this time was different. Earlier, he and Mellie had come together in the heat of a mutual passion. Reckless. Unabashed. Grabbing for what they wanted… wringing every drop of physical sensation from the experience. The sex was some of the best of his life.

And yet now he felt a shift in the force. A ragged tear in the veil of pleasure.

He moved on top, taking Mellie with him by the simple expedient of clamping his arms around her waist as he rolled over and maintaining the connection that made their bodies one. Maybe she *was* tired. But he had the sinking feeling that she had slipped away from him mentally.

He'd never asked about other men in her past. She'd told him it had been a long time since she'd been intimate with anyone, and he had believed her. Now he wished he

had pressed for more details. After all, Mellie had wanted to know about Leslie.

Despite his mental turmoil, his body seized control. Desperately he entered her, again and again, trying to force her into coming with him, but even as he found his release, he knew he was alone in that moment.

Mellie was unnaturally still. He moved to the side and slung an arm over his eyes, feeling ashamed for no good reason he could understand. Why did women have to be so damned complicated?

Was she asleep? Was she hurt?

"Mellie?" He wasn't even touching her hip to hip.

The candle had long since burned out. Her voice in the darkness was small and shaky. "Will you take me home, please?"

Stunned and angry, he reached for the lamp and turned it on. Mellie winced and turned away, but not before he saw her damp eyes. "God, honey, what is it? What's wrong?"

She had the sheet clenched in her fingers, the soft cotton covering her bare breasts. Though she managed to look at him, it was only a fleeting glance. He saw her throat move as she swallowed. "I thought I could be one of those women who has sex as a lark. You know, just for fun. But I don't think I can. I like you, Case. And I respect you. But I really, really don't want to fall in love with you."

The last sentence was flat. He felt much as he had the time a horse kicked him in the chest. No air in his lungs at all. Coupled with a jolt of pain that would have brought him to his knees had he been standing.

What the hell did she want him to say? The days were long gone when he said the *L* word with no thought of the consequences. Hell, he didn't want to fall in love either. Did he?

He was angry and confused and dangerously close to taking her again just to prove how good they were together.

Perhaps he should have talked to her quietly, explained all the reasons she was panicking for nothing. But his limbs still trembled. He'd come hard, out of control, needing everything she had to give.

And now this.

"Fine," he said, the word like glass in his throat. "Put on your dress and I'll drive you home."

He grabbed up his things and carried them across the hall, leaving Mellie the privacy of his room. Alternating between fury and despair, he dressed rapidly and went to stand in the front foyer. He was afraid if he lingered in the hallway, he would bust through the door and drag her into bed again.

Part of him wanted to make promises…anything to get her to stay. But he'd made a fool of himself once over a woman. Any man who let himself be manipulated by female emotions deserved to fall on his ass. That was a young man's lesson.

Case Baxter was older and wiser now.

He had his keys in his hand when Mellie appeared. Her face was pale, her expression composed. But her posture was somehow broken, as if she were leaving the field of battle. Her beautiful dress was rumpled. She carried nothing, not even a purse. He'd been in such a hurry to make love to her they'd left everything in the car when they came in earlier.

"I'm ready," she said.

He opened the door and stepped aside for her to precede him down the steps. Only then did he realize that Mellie's fur wrap lay in a heap on the porch. Neither of them had noticed it fall. They had been too focused on each other to care about inconsequential things.

Mellie bent and picked up the stole, pausing only long enough to drape it around her shoulders and hold it tight. The temperature had plummeted after dark. With her bare toes and all that bare skin, she must be freezing.

"The car heats up quickly," he muttered.

His companion didn't answer. She moved rapidly down the steps, slipped into the passenger seat and closed her own door before he could help. Earlier, the interior of the small sports car had created intimacy. Now it only magnified the gulf between the two adults who had started the evening with such enthusiasm.

In front of Mellie's house he reconsidered. "Do you want to tell me what's really going on?"

Her hands twisted in her lap. "I'm not playing games. Merely having second thoughts. I think tonight scared me a little bit. We've moved so fast I'm feeling wobbly on my feet."

"Are you saying I pressured you?" That thought left a nasty taste in his mouth.

Mellie turned toward him. "Oh, no…no…no… This is about me, not you. It was sweet of you to ask me to the party, and I enjoyed every moment of tonight."

"But you're done."

"Can we call it a strategic time-out?"

"If this is a ploy to secure my interest by playing hard to get, I should tell you it won't work."

Fifteen

Silence fell like a hammer in the wake of his stupid, belligerent remark. Mellie unlocked her door, picked up her tiny purse from the console between the front seats and got out. "I'd like my bag, please." He'd felt winters in the Rockies that were warmer than her icy request.

"Damn it, Mellie. You know I didn't mean that. You're making me crazy."

"My suitcase, please." She stood there like a queen waiting for a peon to do her bidding.

Gritting his teeth, he reached into the backseat and extricated the bag. He pulled up the handle and passed it to her. "It's three a.m. Nothing makes any sense at this hour. Let's talk tomorrow. Dinner. I'll fly us to Dallas in the chopper. You'll love seeing the city from that viewpoint."

She raked a hand through her hair, looking like a weary angel doing battle with a recalcitrant sinner. "I appreciate the invitation, but I can't. And I think it would be best if I

assign another one of my ladies to clean your house. You run with the big dogs, Case. I'm just an ordinary woman who never really believed in the Cinderella story."

"What in the hell does that even mean?"

"I was supposed to clean and organize your house. You got sick. I felt sorry for you. We bonded over chicken soup, and both of us were a little curious. So now we know. Tonight was fun."

"And?" He couldn't believe she was giving him the brush-off. Particularly after the incredible sex they had shared. Didn't she know how rare it was to have that kind of physical connection right off the bat? He'd felt comfortable with her and at the same time eager for more.

"And I think it's best if we stop before things get too intense. You don't even know me, Case. Not really. And I don't know you."

He was too proud to argue. And too self-aware to deny she was telling the truth. When Leslie trashed his life, he had stopped letting so much of himself be vulnerable.

"I'll walk you to the door," he said quietly.

Mellie's brief nod ended the conversation.

Her little house was neatly kept. The front door was recessed at the back of a narrow concrete stoop. In the dark, neither of them saw the obstacle. Mellie stumbled and would have fallen if Case hadn't grabbed her arm.

"What the hell?" His protective instincts kicked into high gear.

Mellie groaned. "Oh, no. It's my father."

The pile of dark clothing on the tiny porch rumbled and moved. Harold Winslow sat up, reeking of whiskey and some other less definable odor. "'Bout time you got home, my girl. Leaving your old pop out in the cold isn't nice."

"Why are you here, Daddy?"

Case noted the total lack of inflection in Mellie's voice.

Harold made it to his feet with Case's assistance. "Came to see you. You weren't here. Didn't have any cash for cab fare to make it home."

"Let's get him inside," Case said in a low voice. "You said your neighbors gossip. Maybe we should keep this quiet before we wake up the whole street."

Once they'd all made it into Mellie's living room and turned on the lights, Case stifled a groan of pained amusement. They were a sad-looking trio. After walking Harold to the sofa and helping him sit down, Case shrugged out of his tux jacket and tossed it on a chair. His shirt was open down the front because he hadn't taken the time to refasten the studs.

Mellie was definitely bedraggled. Her hair was tangled in a just-out-of-bed style that was actually damned appealing. When she looked across the room at him, he had no choice but to go to her and put an arm around her waist. When he touched her, he could feel the trembling she couldn't control.

She lowered her voice. "May I speak with you in private, Case?"

"Of course."

Harold seemed oblivious to any byplay, so Case and Mellie left him to his own devices. In the glare of the fluorescent overhead light in the kitchen, Mellie appeared distraught. "I am so embarrassed," she whispered.

Case shrugged. "Alcoholism is a terrible disease. Have you ever gotten him to an AA meeting?"

"Again and again. But when he's sober, he's the most sensible man in the world. And can argue a person blind. I can't tell you how many times he's convinced me he's absolutely stopped drinking. I'm his daughter. I know him better than anyone. But that's how good he is."

"He's probably able to be convincing because he believes it himself. He believes he can stop anytime he wants to."

"I suppose."

"Would you like me to take him home for you?"

She shook her head slowly. "No. He's my parent. My problem. But thank you for offering. I'm sorry our evening ended this way."

Case leaned against the counter, yawning. "Turns out you had already kind of jacked it up anyway, so no harm done."

Mellie gaped at him and then burst out laughing, which was exactly the response he'd been hoping for. Anything to get that look of sick defeat off her face.

"I can't believe you said that to me, Case Baxter."

"I've been told I have a dark sense of humor." Her smile affected him to an uncomfortable degree. He grimaced. "Will you be okay with him?"

"Yes. He'll sleep it off on the sofa. Maybe tomorrow morning I'll find out why he's here."

"Will you loan him more money?"

Her expression was hunted. "I said I wouldn't."

"It's hard. I know it is." Case brushed her cheek with his thumb. "I don't want to leave you. Hell, I didn't want you to leave my house. You make it feel like a home."

"That's just the furniture polish I use. It probably reminds you of your grandmother."

For a moment he thought she was serious. Then he saw the tiny spark of mischief in her eyes. "Trust me, Mellie. *Nothing* about you reminds me of my grandmother."

He kissed her cheek and hugged her briefly. Nothing more. He didn't want to pressure her, particularly not after the encounter with her father.

By unspoken consent they returned to the living room. Harold was hunched over the remote, squinting at the num-

bers, trying to find a channel he wanted. He looked up when they appeared. "You staying the night?" He addressed his question to Case.

Mellie winced, but Case took the old man's query in stride. "No, sir. I'll say goodbye now."

He took Mellie's hand and dragged her with him to the front door and outside onto the dark stoop. "I'd like to kiss you good-night, Mellie."

"You kissed me in the kitchen."

"Not like that. Like this." Sliding a hand on either side of her neck, he used his thumbs to lift her chin. He brushed her mouth with his...pressed his lips to hers...breathed the air she breathed.

Mellie sighed and went lax in his embrace. Case kept an iron rein on his libido. Now was the time for tenderness. For understanding.

"I do care about you, Case," she whispered, sending his stomach into a free fall. "But we aren't right for each other."

It was not the occasion to argue the point. She met him kiss for kiss, the embrace lasting far longer than he had planned. So long, in fact, that he now had a painful erection with no hope of appeasing his need for her.

It took everything he had to pull away. "Good night, Mellie."

"Good night, Case." She waved as he strode out to his car.

Mellie would rather have done just about anything than walk back inside her house. Harold was a millstone around her neck. As she gave inner voice to that thought for the hundredth time, she felt like a lousy person. Other people's parents had cancer or even worse challenges to face.

At least Harold was healthy. Of course, there was no telling how long his liver would hold out.

Her intention was to walk past her father with a brief good-night. She wanted a hot shower and her own bed. In that order. Harold had pulled this stunt too many times. Even so, she fetched pillows and blankets so he wouldn't have to sleep on the bare sofa.

As she leaned down to pick up her small evening purse, she saw something that made her stomach curl with dread. A billfold. A familiar billfold, half-hidden beneath her father's leg.

"Oh, Daddy. What have you done?"

Her father tried to stare at her haughtily, but the effect was ruined by the fact that his eyes were glazed over. "I don't know what you mean."

Perhaps she might not have recognized the wallet in other circumstances. Many men's wallets were similar. But she had seen this particular one earlier tonight when Case took it out of his pocket to retrieve the coat-check ticket for Mellie's wrap and purse at the club.

"Give me that," she cried. Hands shaking, she flipped open the expensive leather. "How much did you take?"

Harold stood and nearly fell over. "Are you calling your own flesh and blood a thief?" He was wearing a leather jacket that Mellie's mother had given him twenty years ago. The coat no longer buttoned around his expanding waist, but he refused to give it up.

Gritting her teeth, Mellie reached into the nearest pocket of her father's jacket and wanted to bawl like a baby when her hand came back out with a couple of hundred-dollar bills. "Oh, God, Daddy. How could you?"

At that very moment, a knock sounded at her front door. Given the hour, it was a safe bet she knew who it was. She

shoved the bills back in Case's wallet and glared at Harold. "Is there any more?"

She wasn't even sure he heard her. He had dropped back onto the sofa and was sprawled facedown, snoring like a grizzly bear.

Mellie took a deep breath and told herself no harm had been done. She opened the door and managed a smile. "I bet you're looking for this."

Case nodded, his expression relieved. "It must have fallen out of my jacket pocket."

She didn't say a word, and Case didn't seem to notice. He looked past her to the noisy houseguest on her couch. "You sure you don't want me to take him home?"

"We're good," she said, her throat tight.

"Okay. I don't suppose this qualifies for another kiss?"

She shook her head, wanting him to leave so she could fall apart in private. "You've had your quota. Good night, Case."

He sketched a salute and walked away from her a second time, taking part of her heart with him. She closed the door and leaned against it, tears already dripping from her chin.

Tonight was the worst thing she had ever seen her father do. Stealing? Was it a thoughtless crime of opportunity, or was Harold more lost than she realized?

Bracing herself, she searched every pocket on his person. He never even woke up. Thankfully, there was no more money to be found. Maybe this could be chalked up to a near disaster.

In her bedroom, she locked her door for no other reason than that she needed to feel the world was at bay for a few hours. She took a shower and tried not to imagine Case's big gentle hands caressing her body. How could one twenty-four-hour period hold so much joy and heartache in equal measures?

When she tumbled onto her bed and climbed beneath the covers, she clutched the extra pillow to her chest and told herself she didn't have a broken heart.

Not even the pitiful lie could keep her awake anymore.

Sixteen

Case was in a bitch of a mood. Mellie was avoiding him. By phone and in person. It was as if she had up and vanished off the streets of Royal. Four days had passed since the night of the party. On Monday another Keep N Clean employee had shown up bright and early to do the second story of his house. The lady was a pleasant middle-aged woman with a no-nonsense attitude.

He showed her around and gave her carte blanche to carry out the careful list of chores her boss had spelled out. Then he saddled his favorite horse and spent the rest of the day riding his property and brooding about how one ornery redhead had made his life miserable.

Fortunately, he did have a number of things to do at the club. Because of his illness, he was behind in learning his new duties. Gil Addison had blocked off some time on Tuesday to show Case files and paperwork and to intro-

duce him to the young assistant who held court inside the imposing club offices.

Tami knew who got in to see the president and who didn't. She also was extremely efficient and very good at her job. "I'll look forward to working with you," Case said. She smiled politely, already turning back to her desk to resume her work.

Gil nodded. "She'll be the continuity you need, especially if I'm not around to answer questions. But you'll get the rhythm of things pretty quickly."

"I hope I can do the job as well as you have." Gil was a straight-arrow kind of guy, and Case respected the hell out of him.

Gil's careful smile took years off his age. "I'm looking forward to spending some extra time with my family. You'll do a great job as president, Case. Everyone is delighted to have you at the helm."

By midmorning on the Wednesday before Thanksgiving, the club was virtually empty. A lot of people traveled for the holiday, and the ones still in Royal were busy baking and entertaining out-of-town company. Case decided to put in a few hours on the computer and then head home.

He'd have football to watch and movies to enjoy. Lots of men would envy him.

Around eleven o'clock Tami's voice came over the old-fashioned intercom. "Mr. Baxter? There's a Harold Winslow here to see you. He doesn't have an appointment."

Case rubbed the center of his forehead. Surely he owed Mellie this much. "Will you show him in, Tami? I'll give Winslow fifteen minutes. As soon as we're done, you and I can both lock up everything and leave." The club would be shut down from noon today until Friday morning to give employees time to spend with their families.

A couple of minutes later, Tami escorted Harold into Case's small office and excused herself. Case stood and held out his hand, not at all sure Harold would remember Saturday night's fiasco.

Harold grimaced as he shook Case's hand. "Thank you for seeing me on such short notice, Mr. Baxter."

"Please call me Case. And have a seat."

Harold was dressed impeccably today in a sport coat, crisp slacks, and a shirt and tie. The metamorphosis was astonishing. The older man leaned forward, elbows on his knees. "I hope you'll accept an apology for my behavior the last time you saw me. Not my finest hour. But I'm working on it."

Case shrugged. "We all have our issues. What can I do for you today?"

Harold sat back in his chair and crossed his legs. "I've had inquiries from an investor about purchasing this property. So I think it's in your and my best interests to discuss the current lease payments."

"Wait a minute." Case did some quick mental backflips and remembered Nathan telling him that the club sat on land belonging to Winslow Properties. But Case hadn't thought anything about it at the time. He'd assumed there would be legal papers on file somewhere outlining the agreement. Since he didn't know that for sure, he decided to tread carefully. "You're talking about Samson Oil, right?"

Harold's genial smile never faltered. "You've heard of them, I see. Their offer is very generous. But on the other hand, I'd hate to see the club have to move."

Case flinched inwardly. The other man clearly thought he had the upper hand. "I've only just taken over as president," Case said. "I'm still in the process of learning the

ins and outs of the club's operations. I wasn't aware that it was time for contract negotiations."

"My great-grandfather offered this property to the club years ago for a nominal fee. But we've never had more than a gentleman's agreement. This might help." Harold extracted a folded spreadsheet from his inside breast pocket. "Here's the info from my files. The rent over the years has been very reasonable, as you can see. But we're deep into a new century now, and I can't let sentiment overrun my need to turn a profit."

Case studied the figures, his expression impassive. In his chest, his heart pounded a warning rhythm. If there was no written agreement, Harold Winslow had the legal right to increase the lease payments anytime he saw fit.

"According to this schedule," Case said slowly, giving himself time to think, "the rent has seen modest increases every two years. What did you have in mind?"

Harold named a figure that was twenty times the current lease payment. "I realize that's a big jump, and I don't want to make trouble. Still, think about what could happen. If I sell to Samson Oil, they might tear down this building entirely. All that history…gone in a flash."

The threat was not even veiled. Harold Winslow had resorted to blackmail. And Case, who had been the new club president for all of ten minutes, was completely caught off guard.

"I'd have to convene my board," Case said. "To talk this over."

Harold smiled. But the calculating gleam in his eyes told Case this was not a friendly conversation.

"Not much to talk over," Harold said. "Either you accept my terms, or you start looking for a new location to build the club."

"Why would an oil company want land that was checked for oil over a century ago and found dry?"

Harold shrugged. "Don't know. Don't care. I'm a businessman. Money talks."

"And it doesn't bother you that the community might see you as greedy and unsympathetic and run you out of town?"

"Afraid not."

"Royal would never let a new owner move the club from its present location. Have you talked to your daughter about all of this?"

Harold looked him straight in the eye. "Of course I have. Mellie wants money to expand her business. This was her idea."

Direct hit. *Goddamn it.* "How do I know you're telling the truth about that?"

"Women lie all the time. They manipulate you and make you believe what they want you to believe. Ask her how you happened to leave without your wallet the other night. See what she says. I think you'll be surprised."

Case drove back out to the ranch in a daze. Though Nathan had been the one to tell him that Mellie's family owned the land on which the Texas Cattleman's Club sat, Mellie herself had never actually mentioned it. The omission seemed painfully suspicious in light of today's revelations.

And he got even more suspicious when he pulled up in front of his house and found Mellie sitting on the top step.

He got out of the car slowly, his mind racing. Memories of Leslie's lies and machinations filled his throat with bile.

Mellie didn't move. Instead, she waited for him to walk up the staircase. When she patted the seat beside her, he shook his head. "I'll stand. Why are you here, Mellie?"

Her smile faltered. "I was feeling bad about the way we argued the other night. Tomorrow is Thanksgiving. I'm renewing my offer to cook for you."

"No, thanks." He didn't dress up his refusal.

"Am I missing something?" she asked.

"Why didn't you tell me your family owned the land where the TCC sits?"

She had the gall to look puzzled instead of guilty. "It's not a secret. I guess it never came up. Or I thought you already knew."

"And one more question. It wasn't an accident that I lost my billfold at your house Saturday night, was it?"

This time the guilt on her face was clear. His heart shriveled in his chest, even as pain choked him. How could she look so open and sweet and plan to blackmail him?

"My father took it," she said, "while you and I were in the kitchen. When I realized what he had done...after you left, I made him put the money back. That's when you showed up at the door."

"So, to be clear, you chose to protect your father rather than tell me the truth." The incident wasn't such a big thing by itself. But combined with Harold's demand for an exorbitant rental increase, Case had to wonder what other things Mellie had been hiding from him.

Mellie went white, her expression agitated. "It all happened so fast. No harm was done. He does such stupid stuff when he's drinking. I'm really sorry, Case."

"My hat's off to you, Mellie," he said. The pain was gone now, replaced by a raging need to hurt her as much as she had hurt him. "You even told me what you were doing. Winning my trust little by little so you could blackmail me and line your pockets. It makes perfect sense that you turned down my fifty-thousand-dollar offer. You had bigger plans...much bigger."

She stood shakily. Since Case was a few steps below her, they faced each other eye to eye. "You've got this all wrong, Case. I don't want your money."

"Not mine, it seems. But your father just stood in my office and demanded a new Cattleman's Club lease at twenty times the price. Threatened to sell the property out from under us if I don't agree to his terms. You *do* want money. But far more than I was offering. And you don't mind dragging my reputation through the mud to get what you want."

"I'll talk to him," she swore. Ashen and trembling, she was very convincing.

"No more theater," he said. "I know it was your idea. He told me so. The thing is, Mellie, if you hadn't overplayed your hand, you could have ended up with a ring on your finger. I was falling for you. Hard. But I had a narrow escape. You and your dad have a nice little scam going. Maybe you even arranged for him to be on your front porch when I brought you home. I actually felt sorry for you."

She reached for him. "I've been falling for you, too, Case. Please don't let my father ruin what we have."

Her touch burned his arm. Jerking away, he tried not to think about how it felt to rest in her arms. "What we have is *nothing*, Mellie. Nothing at all. You gambled and you lost. Now it's over."

Mellie drove back to town and later didn't remember doing so. She was in shock. In denial. Case had looked at her with such cold fury and contempt she felt dirty.

Her first instinct was to hole up in her little house and hide. Thanksgiving came and went. Her father neither called nor came by. He was avoiding her, no doubt. Only on Friday did she find the strength to do what had to be done.

She went to her father's office and found it empty. But everything she needed was on the computer and written

on notepads in her father's messy scrawl. Rapidly, she made a list of all the property to which the Winslows still held title. At one time, Harold had been one of the largest landowners in downtown Royal.

But in the past two years, he had sold off more and more, leaving him with only a dozen small tracts and two significant parcels of land—the one on which the TCC sat and the slightly larger one outside of town where the Courtyard was located.

After locking up the office, she went to her father's house, where she found him passed out on the sofa. His condition was a reminder that she was doing the right thing. Though she had been prepared to have a knock-down, drag-out confrontation, she left without disturbing him.

Nathan Battle and one very cranky judge were next on her list. Judge Plimpton didn't like being disturbed on the golf course.

Fortunately, Mellie had legal rights. Mellie's mother had left her portion of Winslow Properties to Mellie and not Harold. So although Harold ran the company, Mellie was an equal partner.

By bedtime that night, all her plans had been set in motion.

Case was already regretting his election as club president. What was supposed to be a largely ceremonial title had landed him in a hell of a mess. It was the Tuesday after Thanksgiving, and here he sat in a room with two lawyers and the nine-member board.

One of the lawyers was speaking, shaking his head. "Sadly, Mr. Winslow is on firm ground in this instance as far as I can tell. As he told you, Mr. Baxter, the original lease arrangement from years ago was a gentleman's

agreement with Winslow's ancestor. Unfortunately, sub-
sequent generations saw no reason to add more official
parameters. Gil Addison remembers a conversation with
Harold Winslow at the beginning of his tenure, but at that
time there was only a two percent increase in rent."

One of the board members chimed in. "What if we were
to offer to buy the land from Winslow?"

"With what?" Case had already combed through the
ledgers. "The club has spent quite a bit of capital in the
last few years, first on renovations and more recently to repair tornado damage. The financial bottom line is healthy
but certainly not adequate to purchase a piece of property
this size."

The second lawyer checked his notes. "So what do we
know about this Samson Oil company? Are we sure they
would evict you immediately?"

Case ran a hand inside the back of his collar, feeling
the walls closing in. "We don't know much, unfortunately.
Only that they have been quietly buying up property in
and around Royal…and giving fair prices as far as I can
tell. The thing is, though, a new landowner could choose
to present us with even worse terms than those Winslow
is offering."

Everyone in the room fell silent. Though no one would
blame Case for the current situation, in his gut, he felt
guilty. If he hadn't gotten involved with Melinda Winslow,
she and Harold might never have concocted this scheme
that might possibly cost the club its identity.

The first lawyer reinforced Case's worst fears. "Mr.
Baxter is right. Even if the entire town were to rise up in
protest, there would be nothing to stop a legal landowner
from doing anything and everything with this property.
Without a written lease covenant, we're in murky waters."

Case pressed his temples, a pounding headache build-

ing. To move the club intact was impossible. The history within these walls was the history of Royal itself. It made him sick to think of how much they stood to lose.

"Let's break for lunch," he said. "We'll reconvene at one." In the meantime, he had no choice but to confront Mellie again and persuade her to reconsider.

He was too angry and upset to eat anything at all. So he locked himself in his office and dialed Mellie's cell number. Time after time, his call went to voice mail. Hearing her speak was a knife to the heart.

But she never answered.

When he finally gave up, he rested his head in his hands and tried to think clearly. Mellie knew her father was an alcoholic. Why would she collude with him in such a distasteful maneuver?

Unless he was completely mistaken, and maybe he was, this scheme didn't sound like Mellie at all.

When the lawyers and board members returned, Case was no closer than ever to a solution. He could live with embarrassment. He could even live with the fact that once again a woman had used him for financial gain. What he couldn't bear was knowing that his community had placed their faith in him, and the club might lose everything on Case's watch.

Discussion raged helplessly for three more hours, circling back again and again to the fact that Harold Winslow held all the cards. One by one, each man and woman in the room came to the same conclusion. The Texas Cattleman's Club was facing a crisis as stark and painful in its own way as last year's killer storm.

Suddenly, a knock on the door drew Case to his feet. Tami's smile was apologetic. "I'm so sorry, Mr. Baxter. But this registered letter was just delivered, and it's marked Urgent."

"Thanks, Tami."

Case turned to find the group progressing without him. He had no problem with that. It gave him a chance to tamp down dread before he opened the very official-looking envelope.

He read the brief message once, twice…a third time. All of his instincts went on high alert, looking for a further threat. The document made no sense.

Without explanation, he handed it over to one of the lawyers. Conversation ceased as everyone around the table sensed something of import going on.

The lawyer scanned the contents and showed it to his colleague. Both of them studied the letter before finally looking up wearing smiles. Lawyer number one shook his head. "It seems your problems are over, ladies and gentlemen. According to this, Winslow Properties has agreed— in writing— to keep the current lease price in place for the next five years. And they have no intention of selling the land to Samson Oil or anyone else."

"But why?" One of the board members voiced the bafflement they were all feeling.

The second lawyer folded the letter and handed it back to Case. "Who knows? Maybe there was never really an offer at all. But the point is, the crisis has been averted."

Case frowned. "Why would Harold threaten me and then back down? It doesn't make sense."

Gil Addison shrugged. "Maybe he had second thoughts. Maybe he was drunk when he came up with his plan to gouge the club. Who knows? But that's his signature. So why look a gift horse in the mouth?"

And maybe Mellie had been telling the truth. Maybe she'd had nothing to do with Harold's ploy. Case nodded, but inside, his stomach churned.

The room cleared out quickly after that. Case spoke

briefly with the two legal professionals, making sure there wasn't anything more Case needed to do at the moment. Soon Case was the only one left.

He stood by the window, looking out at the crisp autumn day. Across the street, city workers stood on ladders beginning to hang this year's Christmas decorations on the lampposts.

The momentum of the holiday season was in full swing. Even with all the activity going on up and down the busy thoroughfare, Case saw none of it. The only image burned in his brain was the memory of Mellie's face when he tossed accusations at her.

Good God. What had he done?

He snatched up his keys and strode outside to his car, determined to see Harold Winslow face-to-face and demand the truth. The Winslow Properties offices were open, but inside, no Harold. Only a pleasant thirtysomething receptionist.

"Hello," Case said, giving the woman his most nonthreatening smile. "I'm here to see Harold Winslow."

"He's not here," the woman said. "May I take a message?"

"Do you know when he'll be back?"

"Not for some time, sir. Miss Melinda will be running the business in her father's absence."

"I see."

"Are you by any chance a friend of the family?"

"You could say that."

"Shall I give you her phone number?"

Case swallowed. "I have it. Thanks."

He wandered outside and leaned against the brick facade of the building, his heart in his boots. The enormity of his arrogant blunder stood before him…irredeemable… unforgivable. It was entirely possible he had ruined the

best thing to ever happen to him. And all because he'd been hung up on the fact that his first wife had never really loved him...that when people looked at him, they saw dollar signs and not the man he was.

If the topic of his downfall had been any less personal and painful, he might have been tempted to ask one of his married buddies for advice. But this situation was deeply intimate, and he knew in his heart that Mellie wouldn't want her name and the nature of her relationship with Case bandied about. She was a very private person.

In a few days, it would be December. The nights would grow longer and the days shorter. Christmas cheer would fill the streets of Royal, Texas. But for Case, this holiday season loomed bleak and empty. He'd been given the most precious gift of all...a woman's trust.

And he had thrown it away.

Seventeen

Mellie was exhausted. Running two businesses at the same time required her utmost attention. During the day she bounced back and forth between both offices. At night she fell into bed too wiped out to do more than say her prayers. At the top of the list was an urgent plea that her father was not going to hate her for what she had done.

It had required a concerted effort by a number of people, but Mellie had managed to more or less kidnap her father and check him into a wickedly expensive but highly successful rehab facility about a hundred and fifty miles from Royal.

Her father had been sober and shaky when she left him there. She'd given him an ultimatum. Either dry out and learn how to make a change, or resign himself to the fact that Mellie was going to run the family business and there would be no more handouts for Harold.

The rules at the facility were very strict. For the first

thirty days, Mellie would have no contact at all with her father. It wasn't until later that she realized those rules meant she would be spending Christmas alone.

She had many friends, of course, but she would not intrude during family time. She was a grown woman, and she could get along on her own.

Today was Friday. The letter from her lawyer had been delivered to the Texas Cattleman's Club on Tuesday. Case had to have seen it by now. And yet nothing. Seventy-two hours, with not a peep out of him.

The total lack of communication indicated more clearly than anything else that Case Baxter had no intention of either forgiving Mellie or continuing their relationship. She should have told him right away that her father had taken the wallet. Her lie of omission had caused Case to question her motives...to doubt her sincerity. And he already had trust issues when it came to women.

Mellie's first instinct had been to protect her father, even though he didn't deserve it. But her misstep had cost her dearly.

Gradually, though, as the hours and days passed, her regret changed to anger. Case *should* have trusted her. It had been far too easy for her father to drag her into his little blackmail scheme. If Case had really cared about her, he wouldn't have been so quick to believe Harold's lie. She had given Case her body and her heart and yet it hadn't been enough.

Because he didn't love her.

At the moment, despite her own personal heartache, she was driving out to the Courtyard because Raina Patterson had sent an agitated email asking for a meeting. Apparently, Mellie's indirect reassurances via Raina's cousin had not been enough.

When Mellie pulled up and parked, she was struck again by how charming and appealing this little cluster of studios and shops had turned out to be. Mellie found Raina inside the big red barn, frowning over a cash register receipt.

Raina looked up when the bell over the door tinkled. "Miss Winslow," she said. "Thank you so much for coming to see me."

"It's a beautiful day," Mellie said lightly. "No hardship at all. What can I do for you? In your email you sounded upset."

Raina grimaced. "I don't know quite how to say this because I thought the matter was settled. But I received a letter from your father saying that our rents were going to quadruple. I think it must have come last week, because I found it in a stack of mail on my desk that I had overlooked. He said he had a good offer for this property, but he'd be willing not to sell if we all agreed to the new terms."

Mellie held on to her smile grimly, disguising her utter disgust with her father's methods. "I think I can relieve you on that score. That letter would have been mailed before I checked him into rehab. I'm running the business now, and we have no plans to increase the rent. In fact, you and all the other tenants will receive a registered letter to that effect on Monday from *me*, stating the new terms. I'm sorry my father caused you sleepless nights."

Raina's relief was almost palpable. "Thank you, Miss Winslow. I'm very sorry about your father, but you don't know how much this means." She handed Mellie a small clay pot glazed in shades of ochre and midnight blue. "Please accept this as a thank-you. I think I speak for all the artists here when I say it's hard to make a living via a

creative endeavor. With a stable rent, we'll be able to keep our books in the black."

"The Courtyard shops and the farmers' market are helping make Royal a center for tourism and the arts. What you do is very important. I hope your business will continue to grow."

Though Mellie chatted with Raina for several more minutes, her heart wasn't in the conversation. Eventually, she said her goodbyes and returned to her car.

Though she had reassured the shop owner, it was little consolation for her own situation. She felt as if her whole world had caved in. Even though she had convinced herself that she and Case weren't suited, his lack of faith hurt more than she could have imagined.

Until now she had never understood that heartache could be an actual physical ailment. Remembering the hours she had spent in Case's bed was nothing less than torture. He'd been so gentle with her and at the same time hungry and demanding, drawing a response that stunned her. Until Case she hadn't understood the human body's capacity for pleasure. Sex with Case had opened her eyes to how narrow she had made her life.

It would be a long time before she got over this. A very long time. But perhaps one day she would be given another chance at happiness with a man who was worthy of her heart and her trust.

Grabbing up her purse and briefcase, she got out of the car and stopped dead when she saw Case sitting on her doorstep.

He held up a hand, his expression impassive. "Don't worry. I parked the car two streets over at the grocery store. I know how much you dislike gossip."

She realized he wasn't kidding. Good grief.

It seemed prudent to halt a good six feet away. Her decision-making skills always took a hit when she got too near Case Baxter.

His jaw was shadowed, his eyes sunken with exhaustion. Stress lines she hadn't noticed before bracketed his mouth. "I need to talk to you, Mellie."

She folded her arms across her waist. "So talk."

"Privately. Please."

It seemed dangerous and stupidly hopeful to let him into her house, but she couldn't help it. "Very well."

In her living room it was impossible to forget what had happened in this spot just two weeks before. Humiliation washed over her, reddening her throat and face.

Case must have been affected strongly, as well, because he frowned. "I'd rather not do this here. I have some snacks and a picnic blanket in the car. Will you go for a drive with me?"

"It's chilly outside." She teetered on the edge of uncertainty. Even if Case forgave her and she forgave him, they still weren't suited as a couple. Wouldn't she simply be inviting more heartache if she dragged this out?

Case had his hands shoved in his pockets. His jeans were soft and worn and conformed to his hips and legs like a second skin. His yellow cotton shirt was a button-down with the sleeves rolled up above his broad wrists. "Please, Mellie," he said. "It's important."

"If it's so important, why didn't you talk to me on Tuesday? You did get the letter…right?"

He nodded slowly. "I did. And I went to find your father and demand an explanation."

"But he was gone. My assistant told me you came around asking questions. You didn't try to find *me*, though."

"That's true. I wanted to think about things before I saw you again."

"I checked my father into rehab. And gave him an ultimatum. He blows through money when he drinks, and apparently, he'll stoop to anything to scrape up cash. Including blackmailing good tenants who have never done him any wrong."

"You didn't know what he was doing…"

"No." She grimaced. "And unfortunately, it wasn't only you he targeted."

"So will you come with me so we can talk?"

"If it's that important. But I'd like to change first."

She switched outfits rapidly, going by Case's appearance as a guide and changing into jeans of her own. She grabbed up a scoop-necked sweater in a shade of teal that flattered her pale skin and then slipped her feet into black flats.

A quick check of her face in the mirror, and she was done, though her pulse raced with uncertainty and fear.

When she returned to the living room, Case was standing where she had left him. He didn't smile, even now. In fact, his sober demeanor rattled her quite a bit.

Without speaking, they exited the house and walked for fifteen minutes until they came in sight of an old dusty Land Rover parked at the curb. "This is Betsy," Case said. "She can go anywhere, anytime."

Mellie was glad he hadn't brought the sports car. She'd managed to maintain her composure up until now, but she needed to keep some physical distance between her and Case.

She didn't ask where they were going. That would involve conversation, and apparently, Case was fresh out of that. They drove out toward his ranch, leaving her to won-

der if that wasn't their destination. But Case flew right past the B Hive gate and kept on going.

At last he turned onto a narrow rutted lane. Now it was clear why he'd brought the Rover. Though the tire tracks were deep and well defined, wild grasses growing in the middle dragged at the bottom of the vehicle.

Finally, the car came to a stop. Nearby, a small stream rippled and gurgled. Across the creek, a gentle rise, likely one of the highest places in Royal, drew attention to a single large oak, its branches flung wide in what would be wonderful shade in the summertime.

While Case grabbed up a few items from the back of the vehicle, Mellie shaded her eyes and scanned the area. She couldn't see another soul for miles around. The sense of peace and isolation was stunning.

Case looked her way. "Come on," he said. "I want to show you something."

She followed him toward the creek and across a small bridge. Even then Case didn't take her hand. It was as if he was afraid to touch her.

When they approached the rise, she could see two small tombstones at the top beneath the tree. She and Case climbed the hill, and he spread out the blanket. He indicated the small stone markers. "My mom and dad are buried here. I used to come out and talk to them a lot. Haven't done that much lately. But I wanted you to see this place."

"It's beautiful," she said. "Absolutely perfect." She bit her lip, shivering slightly, though not so much from the cold as from her jangled emotions.

"Mellie…" He stopped, his jaw working.

'What?"

"I am so damn sorry. I never should have believed him. You even told me how convincing he could be. But when

he said that raising the lease price was your idea, I was furious and hurt and—"

"And you thought I had betrayed you."

"Yes." His face reflected grief and sorrow.

"You jumped to that conclusion pretty quickly...almost as if you were expecting me to hurt you."

"It doesn't reflect well on me, but I've had a hard time with women since Leslie. No, that's not exactly it. I've had a hard time with *me*. I have a tendency to be arrogant and in charge, so back then when I let myself be blinded by Leslie's come-ons, it made me doubt myself."

"Your marriage was over a long time ago."

"Yes. But I've never really wanted to be close to another woman until I met you. Suddenly, there you were in my house and in my bed and I couldn't help falling in love with you."

She blinked. "What did you just say?"

"I'm in love with you, Mellie." His smile was lopsided.

"Love doesn't happen so quickly."

Finally, he took her hands in his. "Maybe not for you. But I'm willing to wait."

She wiggled free of his hold, mostly because she wanted so badly to nestle against his chest and feel his heart beating beneath her cheek. She wrapped her arms around her waist, feeling as if she might fly into a million pieces like dandelion seeds dancing on the wind.

"You and I both live in Royal," she said. "Always have... probably always will. And now you're the president of the Cattleman's Club in addition to being one of the wealthiest ranchers in the state. My father will always be my father. He's in rehab, that's true, but you and I both know that the statistics for full recovery aren't stellar."

"What are you saying, Mellie, my love?"

Hearing him say the words brought tears to her eyes and a painful lump to her throat. "I *can't* be in love with you," she said, the words hoarse. "You may not ever be able to trust me completely. And my father may come between us down the road."

Case took Mellie by the wrist and reeled her in. "I'll never doubt you again," he said, utter certainty in his voice. "When we made love to each other, *that* was the real us… no masks, no barriers. We were the only people in that bed. And that's the way it's going to be. You and I against the world. Forever. If you say yes, of course."

His expression let her know that he was not completely sure of her response. Her knees wobbled. "Sex doesn't solve all the problems," she muttered, even as her stomach pitched and rolled.

Case held her close, tipping up her chin so he could settle his lips over hers. "I need you, Mellie," he whispered, his breath warm on her cheek. "Like I need air and food and a place to lay my head at night. I need your wonderful entrepreneurial spirit and your gifts of organization. I need your independence and your work ethic and the way you go above and beyond the call of duty. I need your compassion and your kindness. But most of all, I need your love."

"Oh, Case." He wasn't being fair.

"Oh, Mellie." He mocked her gently as he pulled her down onto the sun-warmed quilt. "Forgive me for doubting you. Make love to me. Let me show you how the world stops when we're together, flesh to flesh, heart to heart."

He waited an eternity for her answer.

"I don't want to rush into anything," she said. "I need us to be sure."

"But do you love me?"

The vulnerability on the face of this big, strong man

broke her heart a little bit. He'd opened himself up to her, had been the first one to speak words of love. It was a pretty good apology…a very nice way of making amends.

"You're everything I've ever looked for in a man, Case," she said. "You're the other half of me."

Eighteen

They undressed each other slowly, shoes first and then the important stuff. The afternoon was chilly, but the heat between them was sufficient. Case shivered when he felt her hands on his bare chest. He'd come so close to killing something wonderful, so close to losing the one person who could make him want more than a bachelor's existence in a big empty house.

With steady hands, he lifted her sweater over her head and then unfastened her bra. Soft, firm breasts filled his hands. "You're beautiful, Mellie."

Big green eyes looked up at him, searching his face as if she expected to find something she didn't like. "Please be sure about this, Case. I can't change who I am… I can't change my father."

He eased her onto her back and undid the snap on her jeans. "You're perfect just the way you are. And Harold will be the only grandparent our children have, so you and

I will just have to keep him on the straight and narrow and make sure he has plenty of little ones to spoil. I want you, Mellie. Now and always."

Her jaw dropped. "Children?"

"Children. Marriage. The whole package. That's what I want. What I need."

He slid his hands inside her pants, dragging them and her underwear down her legs. When she lifted her hips, he eased the tangled clothing away.

Mellie's skin was covered in gooseflesh. He stood and stripped, vowing to warm her up or die trying. He'd be lying if he said he didn't enjoy the way Mellie's eyes widened as she took in the evidence of how much he wanted her.

Seconds later he moved between her thighs and then cursed when he realized he'd forgotten the condom. Mellie laughed softly while he scrambled for his discarded pants and found the item he needed.

And then the waiting was over. He moved in her with his heart burning and his brain marveling that a man could be so clueless about what was important in life.

Mellie wrapped her legs around his waist, taking him deeper, kissing him wildly until neither of them could breathe. Her skin was soft and warm. He felt as if nothing he said or did was enough. He was helpless to make her see what a miracle she had wrought inside him.

He fought for control, even as his body drove mindlessly to a pinnacle that promised physical bliss.

But beneath it all, some tiny rational still-functioning part of his brain noted an important omission. Mellie hadn't said she loved him.

Shoving the thought aside, he concentrated on the feel of her sex as it squeezed him. When he felt the tiny ripples that told him she had reached the end, Case let himself go, giving a muffled shout and burying his face in her shoulder.

* * *

Mellie felt out of control. The contrast to her usual state of mind was sobering. She could barely cobble together a coherent thought, much less a mature, informed opinion about whether or not Case was in his right mind.

She wanted to believe him. She really did. She wanted to plunge headlong into the fairy tale where the girl who sweeps up the cinders meets her prince.

Idly, she stroked Case's hair. It was thick and silky and warm from the sun. His weight was a welcome burden. His body was the only thing tethering her to the ground at the moment.

Case loves me. She said it again inside her head, rolling the three words around and around until she made herself dizzy.

Finally, he moved, rolling over onto one elbow. "I told myself I was going to withhold sex until I got the answer I wanted."

Mellie laughed out loud at the disgruntlement on his handsome face. "Show me a man who can withhold sex, and I'll call Guinness World Records. Besides, what answer are you talking about? I didn't hear any question."

His smile made her stomach curl. "I don't need you to say anything you don't mean, but strictly as a matter of information, do you think you might fall in love with me eventually? Despite the fact that I acted like a giant horse's ass?"

"No." Mellie didn't have to think about it.

Case flinched. "I see."

"You don't see anything, but that's okay, because I like this abjectly groveling version of Case Baxter."

The man growled. He actually growled. "Explain yourself, woman."

His narrow-eyed glare made her shiver. In the best pos-

sible way. She put a hand on his cheek, trying not to fixate on the fact that Case was spectacularly nude. "I won't be *falling* in love with you, because I'm already there. How could I resist a sweet-talking cowboy like you?"

"Say it the right way," he demanded. "Now."

"I. Love. You."

His chest rose and fell. "Well, all right, then." He twisted a lock of her hair around his finger. "We could build out here. A woman should have her own place."

"I love the ranch house, Case. But you keep skipping parts of the script. Either that or I'm getting sunstroke."

"Nobody gets sunstroke in November." He teased her nipple with his fingernail.

Oh, wow. She wet her lips with her tongue. "Was there something else you wanted to ask me?"

"Hmm?" He seemed easily distracted.

"Case? I don't think the president of the Texas Cattleman's Club should live in sin. It sets a bad example."

"Whatever you say, my love."

"Case!"

He flopped over onto his back and spread his arms wide, his big masculine body a thing of beauty under the hot Texas sun. Shielding his eyes with one hand, he gave her the smile that had been her undoing. "Melinda Abigail Winslow…will you marry me?"

"You know my middle name?"

He grabbed her wrist and pulled her down on top of him. "I do…"

She felt him against her, chest to chest, thigh to thigh. "Do you also know that I'm partial to engagement rings?"

"Patience, my love. I have a plan."

She nibbled his ear. "Do tell."

"Tomorrow is December 1," he groaned. The pained

sound evidently had something to do with the way she was rubbing against him.

"Go on."

"I want to spend the entire month making you happy. And I thought we'd start by flying to Paris and picking out an obscenely large solitaire for your left hand."

Mellie reared up in shock? "Paris, France? But you have work to do...and a brand-new position. And I have two businesses to run."

He rubbed her bottom in lazy circles. "Don't say *position*. It gives me ideas."

She scooted away from him and started dragging her clothes on, despite Case's muttered protests. "I think you've had a relapse. We need to get you home. You and I are responsible members of the community. We can't fly off to Paris on a moment's notice."

"You're such a spoilsport."

"One of us has to be practical." When she was decent again, she stood up and stretched, shaking her head to make sure she wasn't dreaming.

Case put his arms around her from behind, a small red leather box in his right hand. "Well, in that case, I guess you'll have to settle for this."

She spun to face him, frowning. "What is that?"

"A ring."

She took the box but refused to open it. "How did you know I'd nix the Paris idea?"

Case shrugged, his smug patronizing smile making her want to smack him or kiss him or both. "I *know* you, Mellie Winslow. And I love every inch of your sensible, hard-working, down-to-earth self."

"You make me sound boring as hell."

"Au contraire, my sexy, beautiful housekeeper. Open the box and you'll see what I think of you."

Mellie was scared. But she opened the box anyway. "Oh, Case…"

"I love how you say that." He kissed her softly and pulled the ring out of its velvet nest. "Give me your hand."

Mellie trembled visibly as Case slid an enormous square-cut emerald onto the appropriate finger. The ring was amazing and exotic. "But this is…" She swallowed hard.

He cradled her in his arms, resting his chin on top of her head. "It's how I see you, Mellie. Stunning. Unique. Incredibly feminine. As precious and rare as the earth itself."

She wiped her nose on his sleeve. "You're a poet," she whispered. "And I never knew. I thought you were bossy and arrogant and—"

He put his hand over her mouth. "We'll work on how to give compliments later."

Without warning, he stepped back and went down on one knee. "I'm going to do this again, just to make sure. Mellie, will you be my wife and make babies with me and create new holiday memories to replace our sad ones? Will you work by my side and warm my bed at night and grow old with me?"

Her face was wet and her heart was bursting. "Yes, Case. All that and more. I love you. Now get up and take me home."

* * * * *

RECLAIMED BY
THE RANCHER

Janice Maynard

One

Not much rattled Jeff Hartley. At twenty-nine, he owned and operated the family ranch where he had grown up during a near-idyllic childhood. His parents had taken early retirement back in the spring and had headed off to a condo on Galveston Bay, leaving their only son to carry on the tradition.

Jeff was a full member of the prestigious Texas Cattleman's Club, a venerable establishment where the movers and shakers of Royal, Texas, met to shoot the breeze and oftentimes conduct business. Jeff prided himself on being mature, efficient, easygoing and practical.

But when he opened his door on a warm October afternoon and saw Lucy Peyton standing on his front porch, it felt as if a bull had kicked him in the chest. First there was the dearth of oxygen, a damned scary feeling. Then the pain set in. After that, he had the impulse to flee before the bull could take another shot.

He stared at his visitor, his gaze as level and dispassionate as he could make it. "I plan to vote Democrat this year. I don't need any magazine subscriptions. And I already have a church home," he said. "But thanks for stopping by."

He almost had the door closed before she spoke. "Jeff. Please. I need to talk to you."

Damn it. How could a woman say his name—one measly syllable—and make his insides go all wonky? Her voice was every bit the same as he remembered. Soft and husky…as if she were on the verge of laryngitis. Or perhaps about to offer some lucky man naughty, unspeakable pleasure in the bedroom.

The sound of eight words, no matter how urgently spoken, shouldn't have made him weak in the knees.

Her looks hadn't changed, either, though she was a bit thinner than he remembered. Her dark brown hair, all one length but parted on the side, brushed her shoulders. Hazel eyes still reminded him of an autumn pond filled with fallen leaves.

She was tall, at least five-eight…and though she was athletic and graceful, she had plenty of curves to add interest to the map. Some of those curves still kept him awake on dark, troubled nights.

"Unless you're here to apologize," he said, his words deliberately curt, "I don't think we have anything to talk about."

When she shoved her shoulder against the door, he had to step back or risk hurting her. Even so, he planted himself in the doorway, drawing a metaphorical line in the sand.

Her eyes widened, even as they flashed with temper. "How *dare* you try to play the wronged party, you *lying, cheating, sonofa*—"

Either she ran out of adjectives, or she suddenly real-

ized that insulting a man was no way to gain entry into his home.

He lifted an eyebrow. "You were saying?"

His mild tone seemed to enrage her further, though to her credit, she managed to swallow whatever additional words trembled on her tongue. Was it bad of him to remember that small pink tongue wetting his— Oh, hell. Now *he* was the one who pulled up short. Nothing stood to be gained by indulging in a sentimental stroll down memory lane.

No tongues. No nothing.

She licked her lips and took a deep, visible breath. "Samson Oil is trying to buy the Peyton ranch."

Two

Lucy was diabetic; she'd been diagnosed as a twelve-year-old. If she didn't take her insulin, she sometimes got the shakes. But nothing like this. Facing the man she had come to see made her tremble from head to toe. And she couldn't seem to stop. No amount of medicine in the world was ever going to cure her fascination with the ornery, immoral, two-faced, spectacularly handsome Jeff Hartley.

At the moment, however, he was her only hope.

"May I come in?" she asked, trying not to notice the way he smelled of leather and lime and warm male skin.

Jeff stared at her long enough to make her think he might actually say no. In the end, however, gentlemanly manners won out. "Ten minutes," he said gruffly. "I have plans later."

If he meant to wound her, his barb was successful… though she would never give him the satisfaction of knowing for sure. As they navigated the few steps into his liv-

ing room and sat down, she found herself swamped with memories. This old farmhouse dated back three generations. It had been lovingly cared for and well preserved.

For one brief second, everything came crashing back: the hours she had spent in this bright, cheerful home, the master bedroom upstairs with the queen-size mattress and double-wedding-ring quilt, the bed Jeff had complained was too small for his six-foot-two frame…

She didn't want to remember. Not at all. Not even the spot in this very room where Jeff Hartley had gone down on one knee and offered her a ring and his heart.

Dredging up reserves of audacity and courage, she ignored the past and cut to the chase. "My cousin is trying to sell his land to Samson Oil." Recently, the outsider company had begun buying up acreage in Royal, Texas, at an alarming rate.

Jeff sat back in a leather armchair and hitched one ankle across the opposite knee, drawing attention to his feet. "Is it a fair offer?"

Nobody Lucy had ever known wore scuffed, hand-tooled cowboy boots as well as Jeff Hartley. At one time she wondered if he slept in the damned things. But then came that memorable evening when he showed her how a woman could take off a man's boots at the end of the day…

Her face heated. She jerked her thoughts back to the present. "More than fair. But that's not the point. The property has been in the Peyton family for almost a century. The farmland has contributed to Maverick County's food supply for decades. Equally important—the wildlife preserve was my grandfather's baby. Samson Oil will ruin everything."

"Why does Kenny want to sell?"

"He's sick of farming. He swears there's nothing for him in Royal anymore. He's decided to move to LA and

try for an acting career. He pointed out that I sold most of my share to him, left for college and then stayed away. He wants his chance. But he needs cash."

"And this is my problem, how?"

Three

Lucy bit her lip until she tasted blood in her mouth. She couldn't afford to let Jeff goad her into losing her temper. It had happened far too easily on his front porch a moment ago. Her only focus right now should be on getting what she needed to stop a bad, bad decision.

It might have helped if Jeff had gotten old and fat in the past two years. But unfortunately, he looked better than ever. Dark blond hair in need of a trim. Piercing green eyes, definitely on the hostile side. And a long, lean body and lazy gait that made grown women sigh with delight whenever he sauntered by.

"I need you to loan me twenty thousand dollars," she blurted out. "The farm is self-supporting, but Kenny doesn't have a lot of liquid assets. He may be bluffing. Even if he's serious, though, twenty grand will get him off my back and send him on his way. He thinks the only

choice he has for coming up with relocation funds is to un-load the farm, but I'm trying to give him another option."

"What will happen to the farm when he goes to the West Coast?"

It was a good question. And one she had wrestled with ever since Kenny told her he wanted to leave town. "I suppose I'll have to come back to Royal and take over. At least until Kenny crashes and burns in California and de-cides to return home."

"You don't have much faith in him, do you?"

She shrugged. "Our fathers were brothers. So we share DNA. But Kenny has always had a problem with focus. Six months ago he wanted to go to vet school. Six months before that he was studying to take the LSAT."

"But you already have a career...right? As a physical trainer? In Austin? That fancy master's degree you earned in sports medicine won't do you much good out on the farm." He didn't even bother to hide the sarcasm.

She wanted to squirm, but she concentrated on breath-ing in and breathing out, relaxing her muscles one set at a time. "Fortunately, mine is the kind of job that's in de-mand. I'm sure they won't hold my exact position, but there will be plenty of similar spots when I go back."

"How long do you think you'll have to stay here in Royal?"

"A few months. A year at the most. Will you loan me the money, or not?"

Jeff scowled. "You've got a lot of balls coming to me for help, Lucy."

"You *owe* me," she said firmly. "And you know it." This man...this beautiful, rugged snake of a man had been re-sponsible for the second worst day of her life.

He sat up and leaned forward, resting his elbows on his knees. His veneer of calm peeled away, leaving a male who

was a little bit frightening. Dark emerald eyes judged her and found her wanting. "I don't *owe* you a single damn thing. You're the one who walked out on our wedding and made me a laughingstock in Royal."

She jumped to her feet, heart pounding. Lord, he made her mad. "Because I caught you at our rehearsal dinner kissing the maid of honor," she yelled.

Four

Something about Lucy's meltdown actually made Jeff feel a little bit better about this confrontation. At least she wasn't indifferent.

"Sit down, Lucy," he said firmly. "If money is going to change hands, I have two conditions."

She did sit, but the motion looked involuntary...as if her knees gave out. "Conditions?"

"It's a lot of money. And besides, why ask me? Me, of all people?"

"You're rich," she said bluntly, her stormy gaze daring him to disagree.

It was true. His bank account was healthy. And sadly, Lucy had no family to turn to, other than her cousin. Lucy's parents and Kenny's had been killed in a boating accident eight years ago. Because of that tragedy, Lucy had a closer relationship with her cousin than one might expect. They were more like siblings, really.

"If my bottom line is good, it's partly because I don't toss money out the window on a whim."

"It wouldn't be a whim, Jeff. I know the way you think. This thing with Samson Oil is surely eating away at you. *Outsiders*. Taking over land that represents the history of Royal. And then doing God knows what with it. Drilling for oil that isn't there. Selling off the dud acres. Shopping malls. Big box stores. Admit it. The thought makes you shudder. You have to be suspicious about why a mysterious oil company is suddenly trying to buy land that was checked for oil years ago."

That was the problem with old girlfriends. They knew a man's weaknesses. "You're not wrong," he said slowly, taken aback that she had pegged him so well. "But in that case, why wouldn't I buy Kenny's land outright? And make sure that it retains its original purpose?"

"Because it's not the honorable thing to do. Kenny will see the light one day soon. And he would be devastated to come back to Royal and have nothing. Besides, that would be a whole lot more money. Twenty thousand is chicken feed to you."

Jeff grimaced. "You must know some damn fine chickens."

Perhaps she understood him better than he wanted to admit, because after laying out her case, she sat quietly, giving him time to sort through the possibilities. Lucy stared at him with hazel eyes that reflected wariness and a hint of grief.

He felt the grief, too. Had wallowed in it for weeks. But a man had to move on with his life. At one time, he'd been absolutely sure he would grow old with this woman. Now he could barely look at her.

"I need to think about it," he said.

Lucy's temper fired again. "Since when do you have

trouble making decisions?" Her hands twisted together in her lap as if she wanted to wrap them around his neck.

"Don't push me, Lucy." He scowled at her. "I'll pick you up out at the farm at five. We'll have dinner, and I'll give you my answer."

Her throat worked. "I don't want to be seen with you."

Five

The barb wasn't unexpected, but it took Jeff's breath momentarily. "The feeling is mutual," he growled. "I'll make reservations in Midland. We'll discuss my terms."

"But that's fifty miles away."

Her visible dismay gave him deep masculine satisfaction. It was time for some payback. Lucy deserved to twist in the wind for what she had done to him. A man's pride was everything.

"Take it or leave it," he said, the words curt.

"I thought you had plans later."

"You let me worry about my calendar, sweetheart."

He watched her flinch at his overt sarcasm. For a moment, he was ashamed of baiting her. But he shored up his anger. Lucy deserved his antagonism and more.

The silence grew in length and breadth, thick with unspoken emotions. If he listened hard enough, he thought he

might even be able to hear the rapid beat of her heart. Like a defenseless animal trapped in a cage of its own making.

"Lucy?" He lifted an eyebrow. "I don't have all day."

"You could write me a check this instant," she protested. "Why make me jump through hoops?"

"Maybe because I can."

He was being a bastard. He knew it. And by the look on Lucy's face, she knew it, as well. But the opportunity to make her bend to his will was irresistible.

The fact that each of them could still elicit strong emotions from the other should have been a red flag. But then again, that was the story of their relationship. Though he and Lucy had grown up in the same town, they hadn't really known each other. Not until she'd come home to Royal for a lengthy visit after college graduation.

Lucy's parents had been dead by then. Instead of bunking with her cousin Kenny, Lucy had stayed with her childhood friend and college roommate, Kirsten. One of Kirsten's friends had thrown a hello-to-summer bash, and that's where Jeff had met the luscious Lucy.

He still remembered the moment she'd walked into the room. It was a case of instant lust…at least on his part. She was exactly the kind of woman he liked…tall, confident, and with a wicked sense of humor. The two of them had found a private corner and flirted for three hours.

A week later, they'd ended up in bed together.

Unfortunately, their whirlwind courtship and speedy five-month trip to the altar had ended in disaster. Ironically, if they had followed through with their wedding, two days from now would have been their anniversary.

Did Lucy realize the bizarre coincidence?

She stood up and walked to the foyer. "I have to go." The words were tossed over her shoulder, as if she couldn't wait to get out of his house.

He shrugged and followed her, putting a hand high on the door to keep her from escaping. "I don't want to make a trip out to the farm for nothing. So don't try standing me up. If you want the money, you'll get it on my terms or not at all."

Six

Lucy hurried to her car, heartsick and panicked. Why had she ever thought she could appeal to Jeff Hartley's sense of right and wrong? The man was a scoundrel. She was so angry with herself…angry for approaching him in the first place, and even angrier that apparently she was still desperately in love with him…despite everything he had done.

During the past two years, she had firmly purged her emotional system of memories connected to Jeff Hartley. Never once did she think of the way his arms pulled her tight against his broad chest. Or the silkiness of his always rumpled hair. At night in bed, she surely didn't remember how wonderful it was to feel him slide on top of her and into her, their breath mingling in ragged gasps and groans of pleasure.

Stupid man. She parked haphazardly at the farm and went in search of her cousin. She found him in the barn repairing a harness.

Kenny looked up when she entered. "Hey, Luce. What's up?"

She plopped down on a bale of hay. "How much would it take for you not to sell the land?"

He frowned. "What do you mean? Are you trying to buy it for yourself?"

"Gosh, no. I'd be a terrible farmer. But I have a gut feeling you'll change your mind down the road. And I'm willing to keep things running while you sow your wild oats. So I'm asking…would twenty grand be enough to bankroll your move to LA and get you started? It would be a loan. You'd have to pay back half eventually, and I'll pay back the other half as a thank-you for not letting go of Peyton land."

The frown grew deeper. "A loan from whom?"

Kenny might pretend to be a goofball when it suited him, but the boy was smart…and he knew his grammar.

"From a friend of mine," she said. "No big deal."

Kenny perched on the bale of hay beside hers and put an arm around her shoulders. "What have you done, Luce?"

She sniffed, trying not to cry. "Made a deal with the devil?"

"Are you asking me or telling me?"

Kenny was two years younger than she was. Most of the time she felt like his mother. But for the moment, it was nice to have someone to lean on. "I think Jeff Hartley is going to loan it to me."

"Hell, no." Kenny jumped to his feet, raking both hands through his hair agitatedly. "The man cheated on you and broke your heart. I won't take his money. We'll think of something else. Or I'll convince you it's okay to sell the farm."

"You'll never convince me of that. What if being an actor doesn't pan out?"

"Do you realize how patronizing you sound, Luce? No offense, but what I want to do is more serious than *sowing wild oats*."

She rubbed her temples with her fingertips. "I shouldn't have said that. I'm sorry."

After a few moments, he went back to repairing the harness. "Why did you go to Jeff, Lucy? Why him?"

Bowing her head, she let the tears fall. "The day after tomorrow would have been our wedding anniversary. Jeff Hartley still owes me for that."

Seven

Jeff made arrangements to have the Hartley Ranch covered, personnel wise, in the event that he didn't return from Midland right away. There was no reason in the world to think that he and Lucy might end up in bed together, but he was a planner. A former Boy Scout. Preparation was second nature to him.

As he went about his business, his mind raced on a far more intimate track. Lucy had betrayed the wedding vows she and Jeff had both written. Before they'd ever made it to the altar. And yet she thought Jeff was the one at fault. Even from the perspective of two years down the road, he was still angry about that.

At four o'clock, he showered and quickly packed a bag. He traveled often for cattle shows and other business-related trips, so he was accustomed to the drill. Then he went online and ordered a variety of items and had them delivered to his favorite hotel.

When he was satisfied that his plans were perfectly in order, he loaded the car, stopped by the bank, and then drove out to the farm. There was at least a fifty-fifty chance Lucy would shut the door in his face. But he was convinced her request for a loan was legit. In order to get the cash, she had to go along with his wishes.

Unfortunately, Kenny answered the door. And he was spoiling for a fight.

Jeff had spent his entire life in Texas. He was no stranger to brawls and the occasional testosterone overload. But if he had plans for himself and Lucy, first he had to get past her gatekeeper. He held up his hands in the universal gesture for noncombative behavior. "I come in peace, big guy."

"Luce never should have asked you for the money. I can manage on my own."

"In LA? I don't think so. Not without liquidating your assets. And that will break your cousin's heart. Is that really what you want to do?"

"You're hardly the man to talk about breaking Lucy's heart." But it was said without heat. As if Kenny understood that more was at stake here than his would-be career.

"Where is she?" Jeff asked. "We need to go."

"I think she was on the phone, but she'll be out soon. Though I sure as hell don't know why."

"Lucy and I have some unfinished business from two years ago. It's time to settle a few scores."

Kenny blanched. "I don't want to be in the middle of this."

"Too late. You shouldn't have tried to sell your land to Samson Oil. And besides, Lucy came to me...not the other way around. What does that tell you?"

Kenny bristled. "It tells me that my cousin cares about me. I have no idea what it says about you."

Eight

Lucy stood just out of sight in the hallway and listened to the two men argue. Strangely, there was not much real anger in the exchange. At one time, Kenny and Jeff had been good friends. Kenny was supposed to walk Lucy down the aisle and hand her over to the rancher who had swept her off her feet. But that moment never happened.

Lucy cleared her throat and eased past Kenny to step onto the porch. "Don't worry if I'm late," she said.

Kenny tugged her wrist and leaned in to kiss her on the cheek. "Text me and let me know your plans. So I don't worry."

His droll attempt to play mother hen made her smile. "Very funny. But yes… I'll be in touch."

At last she had to face Jeff. He stood a few feet away, his expression inscrutable. In a dark tailored suit, with a crisp white dress shirt and blue patterned tie, he looked like a man in charge of his domain. A light breeze ruffled his hair.

His sharp, intimate gaze scanned her from head to toe. "Let's go" was all he said.

Lucy sighed inwardly. So much for her sexy black cocktail dress with spaghetti straps. The daring bodice showcased her cleavage nicely. Big surly rancher barely seemed to notice.

They descended the steps side by side, Jeff's hand on her elbow. He helped her into the car, closed her door and went around to slide into the driver's seat. The car was not one she remembered. But it had all the bells and whistles. It smelled of leather and even more faintly, the essence of the man himself.

For the first ten miles silence reigned. Pastures of cattle whizzed by outside the window, their existence so commonplace, Lucy couldn't pretend a deep interest in the scenery. Instead, she kicked off her shoes, curled her legs beneath her, and leaned forward to turn on the satellite radio.

"Do you mind?" she asked.

Jeff shot her a glance. "Does being alone with me make you nervous, Lucy?"

"Of course not." Her hand hovered over the knob. More than anything else, she wanted music to fill the awkward silence. But if Jeff saw that as a sign of weakness, then she wouldn't do it.

She sat back, biting her bottom lip. Now the silence was worse. Before, they had simply been two near strangers riding down the road. Jeff's deliberately provocative question set her nerves on edge.

"While we're on our way," she said, "why don't you tell me what these conditions are? The ones I have to agree to so you'll loan me the money?"

Jeff didn't answer her question. "I'm curious. Why doesn't Kenny go out and get his own loan?"

"He's shoveled everything he has back into the farm. His credit's maxed out. Besides, his solution is selling to Samson Oil. I explained that."

"True. You did."

"So tell me, Jeff. What do you want from me?"

Nine

What do you want from me? Lucy's frustrated question was one Jeff would have been glad to answer. In detail. Slowly. All night. But first there were hurdles to jump.

Though he kept his hands on the wheel and his eyes on the road, he had already memorized every nuance of his companion's appearance. Everything from her sexy black high heels all the way up to her sleek and shiny hair tucked behind one ear.

Her black cocktail dress, at first glance, was entirely appropriate for dinner in the big city. But damned if he wasn't going to have the urge to take off his jacket and wrap her up in it. He didn't want other men looking at her.

He felt possessive, which was ridiculous, because Lucy was definitely her own woman. If she chose to prance stark naked down Main Street, he couldn't stop her. So maybe he needed to take a different tack entirely. Instead of bossing

her around, perhaps he should use another very enjoyable means of communication.

Right now, she was a hen with ruffled feathers. He had upset her already. The truth was, he didn't care. He'd rather have anger from Lucy than outright indifference.

He could work with anger.

"We'll talk about the specifics over dinner, Lucy. Why don't you relax and tell me about your work in Austin."

His diversion worked for the next half hour. In his peripheral vision, he watched as Lucy's body language went from tense and guarded to normal. Or at least as normal as it could be given the history between them.

Later, when he pulled up in front of the luxury hotel in the heart of the city, Lucy shot him a sharp-eyed glance.

He took her elbow and led her inside. "The restaurant here is phenomenal," he said. "I think you'll enjoy it."

Over appetizers and drinks, Lucy thawed further. "So far, I'm impressed. I forgot to eat lunch today, so I was starving."

Jeff was hungry, too, but he barely tasted the food. He was gambling a hell of a lot on the outcome of this encounter.

They ordered the works…filet and lobster. With spinach salad and crusty rolls. Clearly, Lucy enjoyed her meal. *He* enjoyed the fact that she didn't fuss about calories and instead ate with enthusiasm.

Good food prepared from fresh ingredients was a sensual experience. It tapped into some of the same pleasure centers as lovemaking. It was hard to bicker under the influence of a really exceptional Chablis and a satisfying, special-occasion dinner.

That's what he was counting on…

Lucy declined dessert. Jeff did, as well. As they lin-

gered over coffee, he could practically see her girding her loins for battle.

She stirred a single packet of sugar into her cup and sat back in her chair, eyeing him steadily. "Enough stalling, Jeff. I've come here with you for dinner, which was amazing, I might add. But I need to have your answer. Will you loan me the money, and what are your conditions?"

Ten

Lucy was braced for bad news. It was entirely possible that Jeff had brought her here—wined and dined her—in order to let her down gently. To give her an outright no.

Watching him take a sip of coffee was only one of many mistakes she had made tonight. When his lips made contact with the rim of his thin china cup, she was almost sure the world stood still for a split second. The man had the most amazing mouth. Firm lips that could caress a woman's breast or kiss her senseless in the space of a heartbeat.

Though it had been two long years, Lucy still remembered the taste of his tongue on hers.

"Jeff?" She heard the impatience in her voice. "I asked you a question."

He nodded slowly. "Okay. Hear me out before you run screaming from the room."

Her nape prickled. "I don't understand."

Leaning toward her, he rested his forearms on the table,

hands clasped in front of him. His dark gaze captured hers like a mesmerist. "When you walked out the night before our wedding, we never had closure. I went from being almost married to drastically single so fast it's a wonder I didn't get whiplash."

"What's your point?" Her throat was tight.

"Divorced couples end up back in bed together all the time. Lovers break up and hook up and break up again. I'm curious to see if you and I still have a spark."

Hyperventilation threatened. "We can talk about that later." *Much later.* "You said you had two conditions. What are they?" For the first time tonight, she caught a glimpse of something in his eyes. Was it pain? Or vulnerability? Not likely.

He shrugged. "I want you to ask Kirsten to tell you what really happened that night."

"I don't need to talk to Kirsten. I'm not blind. I saw everything. You kissed her and she kissed you back. Both of you betrayed me. The truth is, Kirsten and I have barely spoken since that night. She has shut me out. I think she's embarrassed that she didn't stop you."

"And you really believe that?"

His tone wasn't sarcastic. If anything, the words were wistful, cajoling. She'd spent two horrid years wondering why the man who professed to love her madly had been such a jerk. Or why Kirsten, her best friend, hadn't punched Jeff in the stomach. She had seen Kirsten's face when Lucy caught them. The other woman had looked shattered. But her arms had definitely been twined about Jeff's neck.

"I don't know what to believe anymore," she muttered. Jeff hadn't dated anyone at all in the last twenty-four months according to Royal's gossipy grapevine. He was a young, virile man in his prime. If he was such a lying,

cheating scoundrel, why hadn't he been out on the town with a dozen women in the interim? "And if I do go talk to Kirsten about what happened? That's it? What about the other requirement?"

Those chiseled lips curved upward in a smile that made her spine tighten and her stomach curl. "I'd like the two of us to go upstairs and spend the night together."

Eleven

Go upstairs and spend the night together.

His words echoed in her brain like tiny pinballs. "You mean sex?"

Jeff laughed out loud, but it was gentle laughter, and his eyes were filled with warmth. "Yes, Lucy. Sex. I've missed you. I've missed us."

Oh, my...

What was a woman supposed to say to that kind of proposition? Especially when it sounded so very appealing. She cleared her throat. "If you're offering to pay me twenty thousand dollars to have sex with you, I think we could both get arrested."

His smile was enigmatic. "Let's not muddy the waters, then. I promise to give you the money for Kenny as long as you have a conversation with Kirsten." He reached across the table and took one of her hands in both of his. When

he rubbed his thumb across her wrist, it was all she could do not to jerk away in a panic.

"Steady, Lucy." His grip tightened. "I think deep in your heart you know the truth. But you're afraid to face it. I understand that. Maybe it will take time. So for tonight, I'm not expecting you to make any sweeping declarations. I'm only asking if you'll be my lover again. One night. For closure. Unless you change your mind and decide you want more."

"Why would I do that?" she asked faintly, remembering all the evenings she had cried herself to sleep.

"You'll have to figure it out for yourself," he said. That same thumb rubbed back and forth across her knuckles.

She seized on one inescapable truth. "But I don't have anything with me to stay overnight," she said, grasping at straws. "And neither do you."

"I brought a bag," he replied calmly. "And I ordered a few items for a female companion. I believe you'll find I've thought of everything you need to be comfortable."

"And you don't think this is at all creepy?" With her free hand she picked up her water glass, intending to take a sip. But her fingers shook so much she set it back down immediately.

Jeff released her, his expression sober. "You're the one who came to see me, not the other way around. If you want me to take you home, all you have to do is say so. But I'm hoping you'll give us this one night to see if the spark is still there."

"Why are you doing this?" she whispered. He was breaking her heart all over again, and she was so damned afraid to trust him. Even worse, she was afraid to trust herself.

Jeff summoned the waiter and dealt with the check. Moments later, the transaction was complete. Jeff stood

and held out his hand. "I need your decision, Lucy." He was tall and sexy and clear-eyed in his resolve. "Shall we go, or shall we stay? It's up to you. It always has been."

Twelve

Jeff's heartbeat thundered in his chest. He wasn't usually much of a gambler, but he was betting on a future that, at the moment, didn't exist.

It was a thousand years before Lucy slid her small hand into his bigger one. "Yes," she said. The word was barely audible.

He led her among the crowded tables and out into the hotel foyer. After tucking her into an elegant wingback chair, he brushed a finger across her cheek. "Stay here. I won't be long."

Perhaps the desk clerk thought him a tad weird. Jeff could barely register for glancing back over his shoulder to see if Lucy had bolted. But all was well. She had her phone in her hand and was apparently checking messages.

When he had the key, he went back for her. "Ready?"

Her face was pale when she looked up at him. But she smiled and rose to her feet. "Yes."

They shared an elevator with three other people. On the seventh floor, Jeff took Lucy's arm and steered her off. "This way," he said gruffly as he located their room number on the brass placard. They were at the end of the hall, far from the noise of the elevator and the ice machine.

He'd booked a suite. Inside the pleasantly neutral sitting room, he took off his jacket and tie. "Would you like more wine?" he asked.

Lucy hovered by the door. "No. Why do you want me to go talk to Kirsten?" Her eyes were huge…perhaps revealing distress over the shambles of their past.

He leaned against the arm of the sofa. "She was your friend from childhood. You and I had dated less than a year. As angry as I was with you, on some level I understood."

"Why were you angry with *me*?" she asked, her expression bewildered. "You were the one who cheated."

He didn't rise to the bait. "It's been two years, Lucy. Two long, frustrating years when you and I should have been starting our life together. Surely you've had time enough to figure it out by now."

"You didn't come after me." Her voice was small, the tone wounded.

Ah…there it was. The evidence of his own stupidity. "You're right about that. I let my pride get in the way. When you wouldn't take my calls, I wanted to make you grovel. But as it turns out, that was an abysmally arrogant and unproductive attitude on my part. I'm sorry I didn't follow you back to Austin. I should have. Maybe one good knock-down, drag-out fight would have cleared the air."

"And now…if I agree to go talk to Kirsten?"

He swallowed the last of his wine and set the glass aside. "I don't want to discuss Kirsten anymore. You and I are the only two people here in this suite. What I desperately need is make love to you."

Thirteen

Lucy sucked in a deep breath, her insides tumbling as they had the one and only time she rode the Tilt-A-Whirl at the county fair. On that occasion, she had tossed her cookies afterward.

Tonight was different. Tonight, the butterflies were all about anticipation and arousal and the rebirth of hope. Why else would she be here with Jeff Hartley?

She nodded, kicking off her shoes. "Yes." There were a million words she wanted to say to him, and not all of them kind. But for some reason, the only thing that mattered at this very moment was feeling the warmth of his skin beneath her fingers one more time.

She felt more emotionally bereft than brave, but she made her feet move…carrying her across the plush carpet until she stood face-to-face with Jeff. His gaze was stormy, his fists were clenched at his sides.

He stared into her eyes as if looking for something he

was afraid he wouldn't find. "God, you're beautiful," he said, his voice hoarse. "I thought I could put you out of my mind, but that was laughable. You've haunted every room in my house. Kiss me, Lucy."

With one of his strong arms around her back, binding her to him, she went up on her tiptoes and found his mouth with hers. The taste of him brought tears to sting her eyelids, but she blinked them back, wanting this moment to be about light and warmth and pleasure. He held her gently as he took everything she thought she knew and stripped it away, leaving only a yearning that was heart-deep and visceral.

She wanted to say something, but Jeff was a man possessed. He found the zipper at her back and lowered it with one smooth move. Then he shimmied the garment down her body and held her arm as she stepped out of the small heap of fabric.

Beneath the dress, she wore lacy underthings. Jeff didn't pause to admire them. The lingerie went the way of the crumpled dress.

Suddenly, she realized that she was completely naked, and her would-be lover was staring. Hotly. Glassy-eyed. As if he'd been struck in the head and was seeing stars.

She crossed her arms over strategic areas and scowled. "Take off your clothes, Mr. Hartley. This show works both ways."

If the situation hadn't been so emotionally fraught, she might have chuckled when Jeff dragged his shirt, still half-buttoned, over his head. His pants and socks and shoes were next in the frenzied disrobing.

Underneath, he wore snug-fitting black boxers that strained to contain his arousal. Suddenly, she felt shy and afraid and clueless. Had she ever really known this man at all?

He didn't give her time for second thoughts. "We'll be more comfortable on the bed," he promised, scooping her up and carrying her through the adjacent doorway. She barely noticed the furnishings or the color scheme. Her gaze was locked on Jeff's face.

His cheekbones were slashed with color. His eyes glittered with lust. "You're mine, Lucy."

Fourteen

The bottom dropped out of her stomach. It was as simple as that. Even if he hadn't said the words, she would have felt his deep conviction in the way he moved his hands over her body.

He still wore his underwear, maybe to keep things from rushing along too rapidly. He was tanned all over from his days of working in the hot sun. His chest was a work of art, sleekly muscled…lightly dusted with golden hair.

Even as she took in the magnificence that was Jeff Hartley, she couldn't help but question his motives. As a rancher and a member of the Texas Cattleman's Club in Royal, he was a well-respected member of the community. Had his reputation suffered when she walked out on him? Was there a part of him that wanted revenge?

He loomed over her on one elbow, his emerald eyes darker than normal, his forehead damp, his skin hot. It was all she could do to be still and let him map her curves

like a blind man. Need rose, hot and tormenting, between her clenched thighs.

How could she want him so desperately while knowing full well there were serious unresolved issues between them? "Jeff," she whispered, not really knowing what to say. "Please…" Despite what her head told her, her heart and her body were in control.

It was as if they had never been apart. He rolled her to her stomach and moved aside a swath of her hair to kiss the nape of her neck. The press of his lips against sensitive skin sent sparkles of sensation all down to her feet.

When he nibbled his way along her spine, her hands grabbed the sheets. He lay heavy against her, his big body weighing her down deliciously.

At last she felt him move away. He scrambled out of his boxers and rolled her to face him once again. She let her arms fall lax above her head, enjoying the way his avid gaze scoured her from head to toe.

It had been two years since she had seen him naked… two years since she had seen him at all. Beginning with what would have been their wedding morning, he had phoned her every single day for a week. Each one of those times she had let his call go to voice mail, telling herself he should have had the guts to face her in person.

Had she wronged him grievously? In her blind hurt, had she rushed to judgment? The enormity of the question made her head spin.

For weeks and months, she had wallowed in her self-righteous anger, calling Jeff Hartley every dirty name in the book, telling herself she hated him…that he was a worthless cad, a two-timing player.

But what if she had been wrong? What if she had been terribly, dreadfully wrong?

He used his thumb to erase the frown lines between her brows. "What's the matter, buttercup?"

Hearing the silly nickname made the lump in her throat grow larger. "I don't know what we're doing, Jeff."

His smile was lopsided, more rueful than happy. "Damned if I know either. But let's worry about that tomorrow."

She cupped his cheek, feeling the light stubble of late-day beard. "Since when do *you* channel Scarlett O'Hara?"

Without answering, he reached in his discarded pants for a condom and took care of business. Then he moved between her thighs. "Put your arms around my neck, Lucy. I want to feel you skin to skin."

Fifteen

Jeff tried to live an honorable life. He gave to charity, offered work to those who needed it, supported his local civic organizations and donated large sums of money to the church where he had been baptized as an infant.

But lying in Lucy's arms, on the brink of restaking a claim that had lain dormant for two years, he would have sold his soul to the devil if he could have frozen time.

Lucy's eyes were closed.

"Look at me," he commanded. "I want you to see my face when I take you."

Her breath came in short, sharp pants. She nodded, her eyelids fluttering upward as she obeyed.

Gently, he spread her thighs and positioned his aching flesh against the moist, pink lips of her sex. When he pushed inside, he was pretty sure he blacked out for a moment. *Two years. Two damn years.*

It was everything he remembered and more. The fragrance of her silky skin. The sound of her soft, incoherent

cries. His body and his soul would have recognized her even in the dark, anywhere in the world.

He felt her heart beating against his chest. Or maybe it was his heart. It was impossible to separate the two. Burying his face in the crook of her shoulder, he moved in her steadily, sucking in a sharp breath when she wrapped her legs around his waist, driving him deeper.

He thrust slowly at first, but all the willpower in the world couldn't stem the tide of his hunger. His body betrayed him, his desire cresting sharply in a release that left him almost insensate.

Lucy hadn't come. He knew that. But his embarrassment was blunted by the sheer euphoria of being with her again. He kissed her cheek. "I'm sorry, love." He touched her gently, intimately, stroking and teasing until she climaxed, too. Afterward, he held her close for long minutes.

But reality eventually intruded.

Lucy reclined on her elbow, head propped on her hand. "May I ask you a very personal question?"

Though his breathing was still far from steady, he nodded. "Anything."

Lucy reached out and smoothed a lock of his hair. Her gaze was troubled. "When was the last time you had sex?"

Here it was. The first test of their tenuous reconciliation. "You should know," he said quietly. "You were there."

She went white, her expression anguished, tears spilling from her eyes and rolling down her cheeks. "You're lying," she whispered.

Her accusation angered him. But he gathered her into his arms and held her as she sobbed. Two years of grief and separation. Two years of lost happiness.

"I know you don't believe me, Lucy." He combed her hair with his fingers. "Maybe you never will. Don't cry so hard. You'll make yourself sick."

Perhaps they should have talked first. But his need for her had obliterated everything else. Now she was distraught, and he didn't know how to help her get to the truth. Was this going to be the only moment they had? If so, he wasn't prepared to let it end so soon.

Feeling her nude body against his healed the raw places inside him. She was his. He would fight. For however long it took. No matter what happened, he was never letting her go again.

Sixteen

Lucy's brain whirled in sickening circles. Jeff wanted her to believe he hadn't been with another woman since she walked out on him. He expected her to believe he had not cheated on her.

She should have been elated…relieved. Instead, she was shattered and confused and overwhelmed. Was she going to be one of those women who blindly accepted whatever her lover told her? Where was her pride? Her intuition? Her intellect?

Jeff was silent, but tense. She knew him well enough to realize that he was angry. Even so, the strong arms holding her close were her only anchors at a moment when everything she thought she knew was shattering into tiny fragments and swirling away.

At last, the storm of grief passed. She lay against him limp with emotional distress. Taking a deep breath, she tried to sit up. "We need to go back to Royal. Right now. I

need to see you and Kirsten in the same room at the same time to hash this out."

Jeff moved up against the headboard. His jaw was tight, but he scooped her into his lap. "It can wait until tomorrow. We deserve this night together, Lucy. You and I. No one else. Even if you don't believe me."

With her cheek against his chest, she seesawed between hope and despair. Was it possible she hadn't lost him after all, or was she being a credulous fool? If she had placed more trust in what they had from the beginning, it might never have come to this. Was it too late to repair the damage and to reclaim the future that had almost been destroyed?

And what if Jeff *had* initiated the kiss with Kirsten? Could she forgive him and move on? Was what they had worth another chance? Would their relationship ever be the same?

She was deeply moved, unbearably regretful, and at the same time giddy with hope. Tipping back her head so she could see his face, she memorized his features. The heavy-lidded green eyes. The strong chin. The slightly crooked nose. The tiny scar below his left cheekbone.

He gazed down at her with a half-smile. "Are we good?"

"I'm not sure." She wanted to say more. She wanted to pour out her heart…to tell him about the endless months of despair and loneliness. But now was not the time to be sad. "Kiss me again," she whispered unsteadily. "So I know this isn't a dream."

Jeff leaned her over his arm and gave her what she asked for, warm and slow…soft and deep. With each fractured sigh on her part and every ragged groan from him, arousal shimmered and spread until every cell of her body pulsed wildly with wanting him. She grabbed handfuls of his hair, trying to drag him closer.

He winced and laughed. "Easy, darlin'. I don't want to go bald just yet."

His trademark humor was one of the things that had attracted her to him in the beginning. That and his broad-shouldered, lanky body.

Before she knew what was happening, he had levered her onto her back and was leaning over her, shaping the curves of her breasts with his fingertips. Her nipples were so sensitive, she could hardly stand for him to touch them.

"I need you inside me again," she pleaded.

"Not yet." His smile was feral. "Have patience, Lucy, love. We've got all night."

Seventeen

Jeff wanted to worship her body and mark it as his and drive her insane with pleasure. It was a tall order for a man still wrung out from his own release. Not that he wasn't ready for another round. He was. He definitely was. His erection throbbed with a hunger that wouldn't be sated anytime soon.

But somehow he had to make Lucy understand.

When he tasted the tips of her breasts, circled the areolas with his tongue, she gasped and arched her back. He pressed her to the mattress and moved south, teasing her belly button before kissing his way down her hips and thighs and legs one at a time. He even spent a few crazy minutes playing with her toes, and this from a man who had never once entertained a foot fetish.

By this point, she was calling him names…pleading for more.

He laughed, but it was a hoarse laugh. He knew the

joke was on him. All his plans to demonstrate how high he could push her evaporated in the driving urge to fill her and erase the memory of every hour that had separated them.

His brain was so fuzzy he only remembered the new condom at the last minute. Once he was ready, he knelt and lifted one of Lucy's legs onto his shoulder. He paused—only a moment—to appreciate the sensual picture she made.

Everything about her was perfect...from the graceful arch of her neck to her narrow waist to the small mole just below her right breast.

He touched her deliberately, stroking the little spot that made her body weep for him. Even though he was gentle and almost lazy in his caress, Lucy climaxed wildly, her release beautiful and real and utterly impossible to resist. "God, I want you," he muttered.

When he thrust inside her, her orgasm hit another peak. The feel of her inner muscles fluttering against his sex drove him to the brink of control. He went still...chest heaving, hips moving restlessly despite his pause.

"Lucy?"

Her teeth dug into her bottom lip. "Yes?"

"I was furious with you for not trusting me. But I never stopped loving you."

"Oh, Jeff..." The look on her face told him she wasn't there yet. She still had doubts. He could wait, maybe. He wanted her to be absolutely sure. For now it was enough to feel...and to know...

Lucy was his.

He retreated and lifted her onto her knees, stuffing pillows beneath her. Her butt was the prettiest thing he'd ever seen, heart-shaped and full. Lucy had bemoaned the curves of her bottom on numerous occasions. Tonight, as

he palmed it and squeezed it and steadied himself against it to enter her again with one firm push, he decided he could spend the rest of his life proving to her how perfect it was.

Leaning forward, he gathered her hair into a ponytail, securing it with his fist and using the grip to turn her head. "Look in the mirror, Lucy. This is us. This is real."

Eighteen

Lucy hadn't even noticed that the dresser was conveniently situated across from the bed…and that the mirror faithfully reflected Jeff's sun-bronzed body and her own paler frame. The carnal image was indelibly imprinted on her brain. As long as she lived, she would never forget this moment.

She closed her eyes and bent her head. Jeff released her hair, letting it fall around her face. Behind her, his harsh breathing was audible. At last, he moved with a muffled shout, slamming into her again and again until he shuddered and moaned and slumped on top of her as they both collapsed onto the mattress.

Minutes later…maybe hours, so skewed was her sense of time, she stirred. In the interim, they had untangled their bodies. Jeff lay flat on his back, one arm flung across his eyes. She snuggled against him, draping her leg across his hairy thigh. "Are you alive?"

"Mmph…"

It wasn't much of a response, but it made her smile.

She danced her fingertips over his rib cage. At one time, he had been very ticklish.

His face scrunched up and he batted her hand away. "Five minutes," he begged, the words slurred. "That's all I need."

"Take your time," she teased. She rested her cheek against his chest, feeling so light with happiness it was a wonder she didn't float up to the ceiling. Maybe she was being naive. Maybe he would hurt her again. But at the moment, none of that seemed to matter.

"You never gave me a chance to explain two years ago," he muttered.

His statement dampened her euphoria. "Would it have mattered? I was desperately hurt and in shock. I'm not sure anything you said would have gotten through to me."

"I deserved a fair hearing, Lucy. We were in a committed relationship, but you were too stubborn to be reasonable."

His eyes were closed, so she couldn't see his expression. But his jaw was tight.

Was it all an act? Jeff playing up his innocence?

There was only one way to know for sure, even if the prospect curled her stomach. "Will you do me a favor?" she asked quietly.

Jeff yawned. "The way I feel right now, you could ask me for the moon and I'd call NASA to help me get it for you."

She reared up on one elbow and gaped. "Why, Jeff Hartley! That was the most romantic thing you've ever said to me."

And there it was again. *Doubt.* Many a woman had been swayed by pretty words.

He chuckled, holding her tightly against his side. "I've had two years to practice," he said. "Prepare to be amazed. But let's not get off track. What's this big favor you need from me?"

"Will you go with me to Kirsten's house?"

His entire body froze. "If it's all the same to you, I'd rather not come anywhere near that woman."

She kissed his bicep. "Please. I have to hear the truth. I know you want me to take you on faith, but I need something more concrete. I need you to understand my doubts, and I need your moral support."

"Damn it. That's what I get for promising you the moon."

Nineteen

The following morning when Lucy woke up, she didn't know where she was. And then it all came back to her in a rush of memories from the night before. She and Jeff Hartley had done naughty things in this huge bed. Naughty, wonderful things.

During the night, he had insisted on holding her close as they slept, though in truth, sleep had been far down the list of their favorite activities. Actually, ranking right below mind-blowing sex were the strawberries and champagne they had ordered from room service at 3:00 a.m.

Jeff was still asleep. She studied him unashamedly, feeling her heart swell with hope and then contract with fear. Loving him once had nearly destroyed her. Could she let herself love him again?

She flinched in surprise when the naked man beneath the covers moved and spoke. "I am not a peep show for your private entertainment," he mumbled.

Reaching beneath the sheet, she took him in her hand. "Are you sure?"

What followed was a very pleasant start to their morning. When they were both rumpled and limp with satisfaction, she poked his arm. "Time to put on some clothes and check out. I want to get this over with."

An hour later, they were on the highway, headed back to Royal. Lucy sat rigid in her seat, her hands clenched in her lap. Layers of dread filled her stomach with each passing mile.

When they reached the fringes of Royal proper, Jeff pulled off on the side of the road and turned to face her. "There's something else I need to tell you."

She blanched. "Oh?"

"Nothing bad," he said hastily, correctly reading her state of mind. "I want you to know that I had my bank transfer twenty thousand dollars to Kenny's account before you and I ever made it to Midland. I wanted you and me to be intimate, but only if you wanted it, too."

Lucy shook her head. "Thank you for that." But even as she said the words, she wondered if his generosity might be a ploy to win her trust...to play the knight in shining armor.

Of course, Jeff knew where Kirsten lived. The party where Jeff and Lucy first connected had been down the street from Kirsten's house. When Jeff parked at the curb, Lucy took a deep breath. "This is it, I guess."

Jeff was at her side as they made their way up the walk. Lucy rang the bell. Kirsten herself opened the door...and upon seeing Lucy and Jeff together, immediately turned the color of milk, her expression distraught. She didn't invite them in. They stood in an awkward trio with the noonday sun beaming down.

Lucy squared her shoulders. "It's been painful having

you treat me so coldly these last two years, Kirsten. But I have to know the truth. If Jeff kissed you and you were seduced into responding, I need to hear you admit it."

Kirsten scowled. "What does the sainted Jeff Hartley have to say about the whole mess? I suppose he's told you what a bitch I am...what a terrible friend."

"Actually, he hasn't said much of anything. The man I knew two years ago wouldn't have cheated on me. But the only other explanation is that my best friend deliberately ruined my wedding."

Kirsten wrapped her arms around her waist, her expression hunted. "Why would I do that?"

"I don't know. But I've run out of scenarios, and I'm damned tired of wondering." Kirsten sneered. "Men are pigs. They want what they can't have. Jeff put the moves on me. He cheated on you."

Suddenly, the pain was as fresh as if the incident had happened yesterday. Seeing Kirsten in Jeff's arms had nearly killed Lucy. But now she had to take one of them on faith. Either her childhood friend or her lover.

She stared at Kirsten. "Did *he* cheat on me? Or did *you*?"

It was a standoff two years in the making. No matter what the answer turned out to be, Lucy lost someone she cared about, someone she loved.

Jeff remained silent during the long, dreadful seconds that elapsed. Time settled into slow motion...

At last, Kirsten's face crumpled. Her eyes flashed with a combination of guilt and anger. "If you'd had more faith in him, nothing I did would have mattered."

Lucy gasped, struck by the truth in the accusation. But her own behavior wasn't on trial at the moment. Shock paralyzed her, despite the part of her that must have accepted

the truth somewhere deep down inside. "So it's true?" Lucy spared one glance at Jeff, but he was stone-faced.

Kirsten shrugged. "It's true. Your precious Jeff is innocent."

Lucy trembled. Knowing was one thing. Hearing it bluntly stated out loud was painful...and baffling. "Why, Kirsten? I have to know why?"

Kirsten was almost defiant now. "I was jealous. Ever since we were kids, things seemed so easy for you. When we came back from college and you hooked up with Jeff at the party, I was furious. I'd had my eye on him for a long time."

Lucy shook her head in disbelief. "You were so popular, Kirsten. I don't even know what you mean."

Kirsten shrugged. "I hoarded my resentment. Everything came to a head the night of your rehearsal dinner. I saw my chance and I took it. I kissed Jeff. Because I knew you were right outside the door. He had nothing to do with it."

"Oh, Kirsten. You were my best friend."

The other woman shook her head. "But not anymore." Quietly, Kirsten closed the door.

Twenty

Jeff took Lucy's arm and steered her back toward the car. "Give her time," he said. "The two of you may get beyond this."

Lucy stared at him. "How can you be so calm?"

He caressed her cheek, his eyes filled with warmth. "I have you back in my life again, Lucy. Nothing can hurt me now."

"Take me home with you, Jeff. Please."

They made the trip in silence. Her thoughts were in shambles. How had she been so wrong about so many things?

In Jeff's living room, she prowled. He leaned a shoulder against the doorframe, his gaze following her around the room. At last, he sighed. "Sometimes we have to put the past behind us, sweetheart. We have to choose to be happy and move on."

At last, Lucy stood in front of him, hands on her hips.

"I love you, too, Jeff. I'm sorry I didn't trust you...that I didn't trust us. Kirsten had been my friend since we were nine years old. When I saw her in your arms, it didn't make sense. So my default was to doubt you. And maybe to doubt myself, too, because I fell in love with you so quickly."

She took a deep breath. "I adore you. I'll suppose I'll have to spend the rest of my life making this up to you."

He pulled her close and kissed her hard, making her heart skip several beats. "Nonsense. We're not going to talk about it again. Today is our new beginning."

Even in the midst of an almost miraculous second chance, Lucy fretted. "There's one more thing."

He scooped her into his arms and carried her to the sofa, sprawling with her in his arms. "Go ahead," he said, his tone resigned.

"I don't want people to gossip about us. Can we please keep this quiet? At least until after Christmas? That will give me time to go back to Austin and turn in my notice. I'll have to sell my condo if I'm coming back to run the farm. I'll convince Kenny to turn down the Samson Oil offer and stick around until the new year."

Jeff's eyes narrowed...giving him the look of a really pissed off cowboy. "No way," he said, his jaw thrust out. "We're getting married this week. I'm not stupid."

She petted his shirtfront. "Then go with me to Austin," she said urgently. "We'll have a quiet wedding at the courthouse. Just you and me. But nobody has to know. I want time for us to be us." She kissed his chin. "You understand, don't you?"

He moved her beneath him on the sofa, unzipping her black pants and toying with the lacy edge of her undies. "As long as you're in my bed every night, I'll do whatever you want, Lucy. But I won't wait to put my ring on your finger."

She linked her arms around his neck, drawing his head down so she could kiss him. "Whatever you say, cowboy. I'm all yours."

* * * * *

COMING NEXT MONTH FROM

HARLEQUIN®

Desire

Available December 1, 2015

#2413 BANE
The Westmorelands • by Brenda Jackson
Rancher and military hero Bane Westmoreland is on a mission to reconnect with the one who got away—his estranged wife. And when the beautiful chemist's discovery puts her in danger, Bane vows to protect her at all costs...

#2414 TRIPLETS UNDER THE TREE
Billionaires and Babies • by Kat Cantrell
A plane crash took his memory. But then billionaire fighter Antonio Cavallari makes it home for the holidays only to discover the triplets he never knew...and their very off-limits, very tempting surrogate mother.

#2415 LONE STAR HOLIDAY PROPOSAL
Texas Cattleman's Club: Lies and Lullabies
by Yvonne Lindsay
At risk of losing her business, single mother Raina Patterson finds solace in the arms of Texas deal-maker Nolan Dane. But does this mysterious stranger have a hidden agenda that will put her heart at even bigger risk?

#2416 A WHITE WEDDING CHRISTMAS
Brides and Belles • by Andrea Laurence
When a cynical wedding planner is forced to work with her teenage crush to plan his sister's Christmas wedding, sparks fly! But will she finally find a happily-ever-after of her own with this second-chance man?

#2417 THE RANCHER'S SECRET SON
Lone Star Legends • by Sara Orwig
For wealthy rancher Nick Milan, hearing the woman he loved and lost tell him he's a daddy is the shock of a lifetime. The revelation could derail his political career...or put the real prize back within tantalizing reach...

#2418 TAKING THE BOSS TO BED
by Joss Wood
After producer Ryan Jackson kisses a stranger to save her from his client's unwanted attentions, he realizes she's actually his newest employee! Faking a relationship is now essential for business, but soon real passion becomes the bottom line...

HDCNM1115